A VERY MERRY XMESS

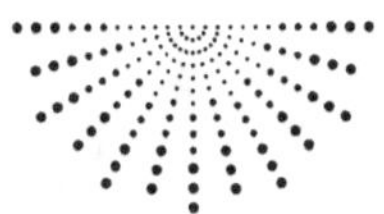

DIANNE JUNE

<u>Trigger Warnings</u>
Strong language
Adult situations
Alcohol Use
Taboo Relationship

Discretion advised.

ISBN: <u>978-1-959253-03-7</u>

First printing, 2022

Silver Fox Ink

*To the women who are unafraid to live in their truth.
The old gals see you.*

DJ

CHAPTER ONE

SILVER BALLS

I hide behind the fluted pillar upstairs after a knock sounds at the front door. My father welcomes a man inside our home dressed in hiking gear and loads of luggage at his feet. He gives him the longest hug I've ever seen my father give another man, and it puzzles me.

"Who is this person showing up right before Christmas?" I say under my breath, staring at him from the balcony above the foyer.

Our eyes meet, and we share a smile. He's unable to take his eyes off of me as I stand high above him in a two-piece sleep set, braless with my nipples growing hard from his gaze.

His smile morphs into a serious grin. I ease back into my bedroom to journal how I'm feeling at this moment—hot and wet to get a front row seat to what's hidden below those layers of insulated rags and corduroy slacks he's covered in.

The way he carries his right leg when he walks, foreshadows he is holding a wondrous endowment.

"Natalia!" my mother calls. "We have company!"

I remove my pen resting between my teeth, imagining it's his cock enjoying a gentle graze on his foreskin, and write my final entry of the night.

'Yes, Mother, we do have company, and I will entertain him.'

The tightest blue jeans in my closet hug my ass, and a fitted emerald green sweater with the words *Ho, Ho, Ho* written in red across my breasts stops short at my waist. I stroll into the dining room.

"I hate that shirt," my mother mutters under her breath.

I grin behind her back and sit across from the gorgeous stranger. "Who's this?" I ask, lowering my lashes at him.

"Natalia, meet my college buddy, Edge Beaumont. Edge, this is my beautiful and talented daughter, Natalia, you've heard me brag about for the last hour."

"The First Violinist." His finger taps his captivating jawline. "So nice to meet you."

He reaches for my hand across the table. His grip is firm, his hands rugged and strong.

"My father has never mentioned you before, or that we were having company," I say, inhaling the wood and mint scented cologne flowing from his wrist.

"Natalia," Mother chastises me. "Don't be rude."

My father interjects, "Edge and I were roommates at school until he decided to backpack across Europe post junior year, and not come home."

"I fell in love," Edge confesses.

"With a girl?" I ask, searching for the label on his dinner attire.

"Not exactly. I fell in love with being outside of America." His face beams like a lamppost.

I slyly exhale my relief, admiring how the purple

and blue plaid design in his shirt mesh well with the tan tone of his skin. A college buddy of my father means he is nineteen years my senior, but he is sexy as hell with a hint of silver specks dressing the black stubble on his chin, and the temple of his face. The five o'clock shadow on his chiseled, square jawline gives him automatic permission to stamp his name on my ass whenever he likes.

My father kills the images reeling in my thoughts and yaps on. "Edge here surprised everyone when he traveled to Switzerland one summer, then stayed there. The last time we saw him was just that. The last time. Until now."

"You've been out of the country this entire time?" I add to the conversation so he'll look at me.

"I've come home a few times over the years for birthdays and events."

"And this year he agreed to meet up with the old gang for a holiday reunion."

Edge looks over at my mother. "Will you be joining us at the dinner, Pera?"

"Even if I were invited I don't think I would go." She shakes her head.

"Sy hasn't invited you?" Edge nudges my father on his shoulder. "What's wrong with you?"

"I did invite her. She doesn't want to admit that she's created this falsehood in her head that being married at an early age kept me from living some grand life." My father huffs.

"But this is a grand life." Edge stands and runs circles with his arms around the room. "Having a family is better than silence greeting you at night...Searching for a connection with stranger after stranger and never feeling complete."

My mother looks away and pretends to arrange the silverware she's already set in perfect lines.

We never talk much about her life before I came along. I never thought for a second she resented having me until this tidbit of information is revealed. If those were her feelings toward me these past eighteen years, she's hid them well, but hearing my father use a private discussion between the two of them with this old friend he was oddly comfortable with made me wonder, *'What parts of themselves did they sacrifice for me?'*

"Dad, did you give up partying and traveling the world with your friend here because of me?"

"Yes," my mother answers before he parts his lips.

"No." Dad peers at my mother. "I could have followed Edge to Europe, but I didn't. Would it have been fun? Sure, but I chose my family. If I had gone, I would have never forgiven myself for leaving you, or your mother behind. You were so little and cute. There wasn't a mountain, or a party, or adventure that would have given me a better view of the world. And, Pera, you are going tomorrow. End of discussion."

Edge pats my father on the back, then nods his head at my mother.

She nods back at him, then rises from the table. "Who's hungry?" Her eyes shift between the three of us.

"Sy has posted some of your cooking on his page. I'm ready to taste whatever you throw at me."

'You don't say?'

"I'll help you, Honey." My father follows my mother into the kitchen."

As the door swings back and forth, and my parents discuss the disagreement with whispers from the kitchen, I stand for no reason at all but to show off my curves. Edge's eyes meet mine.

"So, the violin. Your father tells me you've been offered several scholarships. Am I in the presence of a genius?"

"You are, and I'm not ashamed to brag about my skills. I'm good at *everything* I do." I bend over the table for a champagne glass.

"Is that so?" He gulps aloud. "Will you play something for me–I mean, for us–later on?"

"Trust me when I say, my parents are going to request that I play something special for our guest as soon as dinner is over."

They return to the room carrying hot casserole dishes, a pitcher of water with lemons, and a bottle of red wine.

Dad pops the cork.

"Who is the water for?" I ask, sliding the wine glass I swiped moments ago forward.

"Natalia." My mother side eyes me.

"I'm eighteen, Mom. Let's not pretend I don't partake in a sip when I'm with my friends."

"I suppose it's okay, Honey." My father approves. "She is in the house for the rest of the night."

'That's right, Daddy. There isn't anywhere I need to be for the next few days except home, playing the good hostess.'

Over dinner, Edge explains his success working in tech, and advise my parents how to invest aggressively for an early retirement. He then shares stories of his travels across Europe and Asia. The highs and lows of choosing adventure, and the loneliness of the road.

I grow jealous when he speaks of a woman he almost married in Greece. His voice changes when he speaks of her beauty like she's Helen of Troy, and his eyes glimmer when he calls her name, "Calliope." A name I vow to hate. A woman I promise to make him forget.

Edge compliments my mother on her culinary skills after dinner, and I brush my hips against his arm as I collect his plate. My parents show him to the study as I stay behind to clear the table. He looks back at me, grinning from the side of his mouth, gazing at my begging for attention nipples sitting upright.

"Hello," they say to him.

He licks his lips and I can already feel his schlong piercing the apex of my thighs, blessing my underserved, aching pussy.

As I forewarned, my parents insist that I recite a song for our houseguest. I strut past him before I set up, pretending not to notice his gray eyes trailing my every calculated move, gleaming at my stacked C cups falling forward when I lean over—but I do. And I like his eyes on me.

I wow them with my rendition of a popular jazz classic, receiving applause and a standing ovation that compels my cheeks to rosette. I turn on the radio, then pause packing up my instrument as my parents dance across the room while Edge and I watch them gaze into each other's eyes until ours do the same.

Arousal overcomes me, and I lift my violin and place the scroll in my mouth. Edge adjusts himself on the sofa then looks away. I wait for him to look back in my direction.

When he can no longer fight the lust building inside of him, I gently run my fingers around the peg and lick the wooden neck of my violin. He grabs the orange velvet pillow next to him and covers his lap. I smirk at him, then excuse myself back to my room to add an extra entry in my diary for the evening.

'I want to fuck this man so badly, my walls clench at the thought of him grinding his dick deep inside my pussy. Natalia, do this for yourself. Live with no regrets,' I write, then call it a night.

Wet dreams of the beautiful stranger sodden my panties when I wake. I shower and run downstairs to an empty house with a cold breakfast sitting on the stove.

Popping a cube of honeydew in my mouth, I lean against the counter, to plan out my day.

⸎

A NIPPY ILLINOIS breeze dries my skin on the walk over to Lily's house, my best friend since grade school. Mr. Palmer invites me inside from the cold and takes my coat. I stare at him longer than I have in the past, and compare his mannerisms, his smile, his bad jokes, and old man style of dress to Edge. Nothing about him interests me. He and my dad are both the same age of the hot stranger sensually stimulating my dreams, but something enchanting about him stands out from the older gentlemen of his time, and I must have him.

Lily closes the door to her room. "We should have gone to the mountains with our friends this weekend. I bet everyone is hooking up, and having a better time than us stuck at home brunette losers."

"It's not too late. You can still go."

"What do you mean, I can go? As in alone? To watch my crush and my ex humiliate me. I need a man to throw in their faces to level the score."

"Which is why we didn't need to go."

"I feel like you're calm, even though Dante is up there too with the Second Chair in strings."

"Exactly. She's second. Yet again."

Lily's eyes widen at my quip. She leans back and holds her neck as if she's clutching pearls and smiles. "Can I have some of that maturity and not give a fuck attitude please, because I'm pissed two of the men I have feelings for are not with me for the holidays."

I chuckle and pretend I have a crystal ball in front of me. "Lily Palmer, I predict you will have a harem of men when you go to college in the fall. I see three athletes and a scholar in your midst, and they will fill the void of you hooking up with high school boys this Christmas."

Lily snorts out a laugh and her big boobs jiggle in her v-neck sweater. "I definitely know something is up with you. Spill it."

"Nothing is up. I swear. I don't care what Dante is doing, and you shouldn't care what Frick and Frack are doing. I'm just ready to get out of this town and see the world. Meet new...more interesting people."

"Have you made a decision? Please say we're going to the same college, and I can put you down as my roommate and be done with the process."

"Unfortunately, I am not following you to State."

"Then where?"

"I've narrowed it down to three schools and two states. New York or California."

"Sounds like after the summer we won't see each other until Christmas next year."

"Maybe." I raise a brow at her. "You might blow off everyone for your gang of gut smushers you're recruiting in the fall."

She hits my arm with a pillow. "Stop with that. Unless you really are a psychic. Are you?"

"No, I'm not. And I only dropped by because you

haven't called me in two days. I thought you were being sneaky and slipped up to the mountains without me."

Lily bites her lip. "The thought did cross my mind."

"Maybe I am a psychic."

We laugh and she walks me back downstairs.

I grab my coat and shudder in the cold on the walk back to my house. Tim McGraw singing *Over and Over Again,* and the smell of tobacco hits my nose as the frost on it stings the inside of my nostrils from the sudden transition into warmth.

Edge and my father sit in his study smoking stogies while the clanging and slinging of dishes in the kitchen suddenly quiet.

"Nat! I could use some help in here!" Mom calls me.

"Yes, ma'am," I answer, hanging my coat on the rack.

My legs tremble, and my back feels a chill while my chest heaves a throbbing sensation. I want to slip inside the study and get a glance at Edge blowing smoke, but the bass of the tune, and the echoes of their laughter through the walls as he and my father reminisce about their good ole days briefly satisfy the desire I have to be in his company.

"Where were you?" my mother asks.

"Lily's house. Where were you guys? The house was empty when I woke up."

"Your father insisted we take Edge to see the new development. It is his biggest achievement since starting his own firm. If there is one thing I need to teach you about men, it's let them bask in the glory of their achievements, and enjoy their shiny new toys. Their egos are in constant need of a good stroke."

I focus on the word stroke and nod at my mother's wisdom. She hands me the lid to a container and instructs me to cover the muffins.

"Place them under the glass cake stand. Pack up the leftovers you didn't eat from this morning, and put them on the table. I'll drop them off when I go shopping for a new dress to wear tonight."

"No disrespect mom, but you would have been crazy not to go with Dad tonight. Those old bitches from college need to see how hot his wife is. I've seen how my teachers look at him. You better protect your merchandise."

"Natalia, I don't like when you talk like that. It's not ladylike." She sighs. "Do you really think I'm hot?"

I kiss her cheek. "Buy something low cut, and nothing less than 3 inches on your stems."

I run upstairs and live out a full fantasy in my journal as the music from the den puts thoughts in my head of living in New York, and catching flights to Europe on the weekends to spend time with Edge.

My infatuation and investment in a grown man who did well to avoid me since sticking my violin in my mouth like a weird, naughty, little girl brings a chuckle to my lips. *'I hope he likes weird, naughty little girls,'* I pen on the last line as my thoughts flash of him spanking me with my bow.

The music stops downstairs, and the front door of the house slams shut. I sneak to the window, ease the edge of the curtain open, and peep through the blinds. My father's car drives off in a hurry.

My breath skips and my pussy throbs. The silence in the house stirs me anxious and impatient. I wait to hear a sound. Any sound throughout the house. A crack from the heating unit. A creak in the wall. A cough in the distance. Footsteps on the stairs.

My body tells me to check the house. My head tells me to stay in my room.

I open my bedroom door and there stands Edge. All six feet of him looking down at me like a fucking hot male model posing for a gentleman's winter clothing line.

A raspy whisper of my name ignites me. "Natalia."

His lips part wide enough for me to shove my tongue inside his mouth. Butterflies bounce around in my stomach as hunger pains churn like an Amish butter factory.

"Natalia, what was that last night?" he asks, gazing into my eyes.

I feel crossed, like a school girl about to be punished for misbehaving in class. *Punish me Mr. Beaumont,* is all that comes to mind when he says my name with such authority.

On the other hand, I feel scared he'll punish my integrity and chastise me for being so forward.

The beat of my heart thumps loud against my chest as I stare into his gray eyes and sigh. "That was—me. Me, seeing if I was right about you," I say, rubbing my damp palms against my pants. "Where did my father run off to?"

"Your mother's car got stuck in some mud and snow."

"Why didn't you go with him?"

"I offered, but he insisted I get some rest before our event tonight. I was glad he left me behind."

"I'm surprised he left you here." I exhale deeply. "You know. With me."

"I don't think he heard you come in. But I knew you were home. I saw you come up here when I grabbed something from my room."

"And now here you are, standing at my door."

"Here I am. Wondering what that pretty mouth

tastes like."

"Is that all you've wondered about tasting?"

"Wouldn't you like to know." He steps inside my room.

"Perhaps." I take a step backwards. "I could have been testing you."

"Is that so, Natalia?" He grins, purposely saying my name in a manner to make my pussy pulse. "Then tell me, have I passed or failed this test?"

"That depends. Did you dream about me last night?"

He roams around my room then looks back at me. His eyes shift from mine and down to my breast. They blossom through my bra and point at him like two dials begging to be turned.

He grins and wanders into my bathroom. The click of the light switch pops, and I shudder as he lifts my hamper, and rummages through the bin. He raises his hand with the panties I had on last night dangling from the tip of his fingers.

Placing them to his nose, he inhales a whiff. "I see we dreamed of each other last night," he says, tucking them in his back pocket.

I tremble from my thighs down to my toes.

He approaches me, and I swallow hard, ready to feel his lips pressed against mine. "Tell me about this dream," he orders.

I stumble on my words, looking for the correct way to explain.

He strokes my cheek with his finger. "Take your time."

My eyes close. "We're in Italy at a café enjoying a bottle of wine, overlooking a vineyard in the pit of a hillside covered in white lilies. You pay the check, and we stroll down a path past the bins where they crush the grapes, and enter into a secluded maze of fresh cut hedges. I run from you and hide in the maze. When you find me I'm nude, posed against a water fountain. Your lips taste mine then I drop to my knees. I unbuckle your pants with my teeth and fill my mouth with your cock. You hiss and sigh until you can no longer tolerate the teasing of my tongue, then turn me around and fuck me hard while I hold onto the bushes, and pull leaves from the branches. A worker stumbles upon us and giggles. We carry on while she watches and explosively come together, then the worker slithers away."

Edge's finger leaves my cheek and stops on the lower point of my chin. He kisses me delicately and pulls away.

"I can't fuck an eighteen year old," he whispers. My eyes open and his gray beauties gaze into mine. "It wouldn't be right."

My hands press against his chest. "But I want you."

"You're not ready." He kisses my chin.

"How do you know?"

"Because you're eighteen, and I'm too much for you."

"But you can teach me," I beg.

"Damn, you're making this hard for me."

I lower my hands to his cock and squeeze the knot engorged behind his zipper. "It sure is," I say, running circles around it with my palm. I hope he changes his mind as I entice him with a gentle tug on his sack. "Tell me what you dreamt last night," I demand.

"I'd rather show you than tell you. Be patient, Sweet Girl."

A chill jitters down my spine. "Call me that again."

"What? Sweet Girl?"

"Yes."

Edge swipes my hand away from his dick. "Oh, my sweet girl. When we do fuck, you're going to enjoy every moment of it, and I will take pleasure defiling your wanton need."

"Why not right now?" I pant in his mouth.

"Because what I visualized in my dreams took time. Something we don't have right now. *And*, you're eighteen."

Egregiously I grip on his sweater and lift the hem above his waste. My fingers trace the lines of his abs, and sweep across his back.

"Tell me you don't want me, and I'll back off right now."

"Oh, I want you Sweet Girl."

"Then fuck me, Mr. Beaumont."

"I will. Just not now, Sweetheart."

"Then when?"

"When you're twenty."

"That's eighteen months from now," I say, then stick his hand down the front of my leggings. "See how wet I am for you."

Edge flicks my clit with his finger, then adds a second finger, pressing my clit hard until I wiggle and my thighs tighten. "Promise to keep it tight for me, Sweet Girl." He sighs, sticking his fingers deep inside.

I breathe heavily while squeezing his shoulders, wanting his cock to thrust me exactly the way his fingers toured my flesh.

His thumb presses against my clit while his fingers fuck my pussy. My shoulders lock, and I come on his hand, moaning from the pleasure I know he can bring me.

Edge eases his hand from my cave, then rubs my exterior softly, spreading the mess I've made around my folds. He removes his hand from my pants then places two fingertips in his mouth, closes his eyes and hums as his lips wrap around them.

"It better taste like this when it's time for you to give yourself to me," he says, then puts those same fingers into my mouth. "From now on, when you finger paint, I want you to taste your pussy after you've come."

I nod. "Yes, Mr. Beaumont."

"Good girl."

Slowly, he slides his fingers from between my lips, down to my chin. He lifts it, then hovers his lips close to mine. His tongue draws mine into his mouth, and fervently wrestles me rowdy. I hold onto him while it lasts, then he disappears from my room.

I lay on my bed, squealing internally, holding my pussy with both hands between my legs. I taste my juice and his mouth when I exhale, and savor our combination for hours.

◊

HOURS LATER, he returns from the reunion. I listen to his deep voice laugh with my parents before closing his room door, then his words replay in my head.

"When you're twenty."

I'm frenzied, and want to burst into his room and straddle his cock with my panties muffling his screams. The yearning burden he's left me with is too much to bear on this cold night with him in close quarters, and his big dick that belongs inside of me.

I feel weak for his touch as the spoiled and stubborn side of me refuses to wait so long to give myself to him, and I make an executive decision to give Edge an offer he can't refuse after hours of tossing and turning.

I strip out of my sleep set and ease down the stairs, careful not to trip on my robe hanging at my feet. The door to my parent's room opens as I take a step toward his room. I spin on my toes and rush into the kitchen.

"What are you doing up?" my mother asks.

"I forgot to take a bottle of water with me to bed," I stammer. "Don't forget, I get final approval of all of your holiday looks from now on. Okay?"

She smiles and hands me the last cold bottle from the crisper. "Of course." She squeezes my cheek. "Come on. Let's go up."

I lean against my door and exhale, then chuckle to myself at the adrenaline running through my veins.

I sleep soundly after nearly being caught. The sun brightens my room and I run downstairs wearing a tight house suit, expecting Edge's handsome face to greet me at the breakfast table.

"How was the reunion?" I ask my giddy parents, making eyes at one another above the brim of their coffee mugs.

"It was lovely," my mother answers with the news-paper in her hand.

"A great way to bring in Christmas." My father smiles at my mother.

"Where's your friend?"

"Ugh, Edge is off to see his family in town before he leaves for New York."

"What's in New York?"

"One of his many bachelor pads I suppose."

Mom flips the page of her newspaper. Her eyes grow big at one of the sale ads. "Nat, sweetie, have you decided what you want for Christmas this year?"

"I have." I grin to myself.

I want Edge Beaumont.

Throughout my senior year, Edge Finger Fucking Beaumont became a fantasy I convinced myself I dreamed of during Christmas break. Then, on Valentine's Day, he sent me a poem mailed inside a college brochure, and the fantasy once again was reborn.

I was exposed to a mature world of communication. Love letters hidden inside music magazine subscriptions, sometimes naughty word game hunts with letters circled in pink hidden inside the articles, and advertisement pages that spelled my name and "Taste that sweet cunt" in code.

I masturbated so much during the final semester that I began bringing clean panties with me to school. The urge to be fucked took ownership of my body. Dads who visited the school with Edge's build sent me spiraling into the stall of the bathroom of the back hall, biting my fist as I rubbed my clit to temporary satisfaction, then tasted my essence like Edge told me to.

CHAPTER TWO

HIS PRESENCE IN HIS ABSENCE

The day before graduation, the urge to pleasure myself overpowers me. I slip to the ladies room down the back hall of the gym, my haven and special pleasuring zone, to take care of my needs, wash my hands, then jump back at Dante's face standing less than an inch from mine when I open the entrance door.

"Go back inside. I can take care of that for you." He smirks.

I shove him aside. "I have no idea what you're talking about."

He grabs my hand and places it in front of his nose. "The school soap isn't strong enough to get that scent out. Come on. Nobody will know we're in here."

"I have a better idea. Grow up. When you do that, come by my house, and I'll let you taste this pussy to moisturize those dry lips." I stick my finger in his mouth and swirl it against his tongue.

He grips it with his teeth and smiles. "Shit, tell your mom I'm coming over for dinner tonight."

"I was joking, D. Don't come to my house."

"Oh, I'm coming. And so will you." He grunts. "Your

mom will be happy to see me. She loves me, remember?"

I roll my eyes and sigh. "Get over yourself."

A MINUTE BEFORE EIGHT O'CLOCK, the doorbell rings. I chuckle to myself when my father announces Dante has stopped by to visit.

Goofy and sweating profusely like he ran to my house from fear of being late, he stands next to my father, winning my mom over by flashing his teeth at her, and playing on her love of him.

"You are a sight for sore eyes, Dante. I was upset with this one when she told us you two parted ways."

His hands cross his chest. "Not as much as I was, Mrs. Sutton."

"Are you excited about tomorrow?"

"Yes, ma'am, but not what comes after."

My mother scowls. "What comes after?"

"According to my father, bills, hypertension, and constant worry about losing your hair."

My parents eat up that rehearsed line. The scene of them laughing together like old times irks me. I'm quickly reminded of how heartbroken my mother was when I lied to her, concealing the true reason we split.

I told her we called it quits because Dante's lacrosse practice, and my orchestra rehearsals were too much to handle. She'd think less of him if I told her *I* ended the relationship because I overheard his mother call *us* blue voting trash, and couldn't wait for him to go to college and meet a girl she could be proud to say was dating her son. She'd think even less of *him* if I were to spill that Dante didn't defend me, and left me sitting quietly in his room humiliated until his mother went to bed.

Unlike my mother's kind spirit, I didn't ignore Dante's bitch of a mother's elitism. Instead, I summoned my vengeful spirit, and sent roses to their house the next day.

The card attached read:

> "Piper, I can't stop thinking
> about the other night.
> I promise we'll be together
> soon." ~ Love, Christopher.

DANTE'S MOTHER'S NAME IS ALEXIS.

After putting an end to the pretentious reunion carrying on in the den, I show Dante the door.

He zips up his jacket and blows a white cloud from his mouth. "So that's it? I show up here, trying to win you back, and this is how you treat me?"

"I told you not to come here."

He exhales sharply. "Grab your coat and sit with me in the car for a minute."

I shake my head side to side. "We have a long day tomorrow. See you at school."

EVERY FREE MOMENT I look up, Dante is staring at me as we march in line for our ceremony. His puppy eyes beg for a pity fuck. Eventually, I smile at him, then regret it immediately when his eyes fill with glee and hope.

I know he just wants to get laid. So do I after months of fingering myself to a wicked, wet dream, but *he* isn't the man I want shagging me on a rooftop butt naked under the stars.

His begging eyes are easily ignored when Edge texts my phone with the address of a hotel near the highway exit a few miles away from my school.

> Congratulations, Sweet Girl. Go to the address and tell the clerk your name at the front desk.

I torture myself to get through post-graduation dinner and pictures, half-smiling my way through the afternoon.

Finally, I break free of my parents and visiting family, hours after walking across the stage. The hotel clerk hands me a green and white decorated box, and a key for room 1102. I carry my gift with clammy palms and a racing heart to the elevator. My chest pounds as I plead for it to climb to the top floor faster.

I'm ready to see the face of my silver fox. Ready to be held in his arms. Ready to be freed from the trapped desires I envision night after night.

I open the door to an empty room. There's no sign of Edge. No luggage, or lingering scent of his cologne.

A flashing light blinks on the telephone centered on the nightstand. I press play and get chills listening to Edge's voice speak on the message.

"I know you wanted me to be there today. Since I was unable to fly into the country and celebrate your big day, I thought I would answer the question you asked me that day in your room.

The night we met, I dreamed I whisked you away to a private island in the Maldives. Your luminous skin glowed like the stars in the sky, and your eyes glimmered brighter than the moon pulling in the tide.

I kissed your sweet lips, and you placed your arms around me. I carried you to a blanket lying on the sand and undressed you. Your delicate pants disappeared in the night as I ravished your body into submission. Your legs shivered from my touch. Your sweet cunt exploded with cream around my cock.

I pulled it out of your pulsing pussy and crawled above you on my knees, then shot my glory in your mouth. When I woke, my cock was harder than a bull's horn.

Now climb on the bed, and picture my cock fucking that pretty mouth of yours. Stick four fingers in that sweet pussy waiting for the pounding of her life, and fuck it like I'm there watching you. I wish I was. When you're done, open your present if you haven't already."

Congratulations, My Sweet Girl
One Year To Go

As I follow his instructions, I listen to his message over and over, coming to the sound of his voice. I come so hard, I'm forced to take a breather, and relax on the bed, holding my outer folds as my juice drips on the comforter below.

After my heart rate slows down, and my tight legs loosen from the orgasmic tension from fingering myself, I open my gift. An investment portfolio, and a list of company stocks in my name sit inside a folder on top of a black envelope with an open air ticket valued at five thousand dollars.

Silly me takes it as an invitation he wants me to come to him, but the final gift in the box verifies I've gotten my hopes up, like always. A framed note with the words, **'Til Twenty'** in bold behind the glass reminds me I have to be patient.

I collect myself and my box, exit the hotel, then sit in my car, not ready to face my family and the badgering of my school choice.

I call Dante. "How soon can you be at The Windy?" I ask before he says hello.

"Twenty minutes."

"Room 1102. The clock starts now." I hang up and go back inside.

Early and eager he arrives. He follows me to the middle of the room where I lift my leg, and place it on the foot of the bed to raise my skirt above my love line.

Dante licks his lips. "Where are your panties?"

"I didn't invite you here to talk."

"Nat, I don't know what's gotten into you, but I like it."

"Show me," I say, luring him closer with my fingers.

He dives to his knees and licks my slit. "Mmm. I've been dreaming of this smell for two days." He licks my pussy twice like a cat tasting its milk.

I place my hand to the back of his head and shove his face to my surface. He mumbles inaudibly, rubbing his nose against my clit while I restrict him of air. His lips nibble my folds as I wind my hips forward.

"Aah." I expel, holding his head steady to apply pressure.

Dante's tongue slides inside, and my head falls back. His hands rise from the back of my knees, cuffing my ass so I don't fall back. Slow and hard he rolls his neck so the force of his lips and nose press firm, covering my clit from the top to the bottom.

Light pattering taps from his tongue grace my ears as he slurps the cream from the inside of my walls, teasing me to want more. I back away and smile at him, then push his back to the bottom of the bed. He looks up at me and licks his lips clean. I throw my leg across him, push his head back on the bed, and straddle his face.

My hips ride round and round until I find the sweet spot. His full lips cup my pussy with a tight hold until I shimmy side to side and place the tip of his nose inside my slit.

Dante's hands palm my ass with a tight grip, and I ride his face harder and harder until his nose slips out and shifts north. His tongue trolls around my orifice, searching for my entrance, then makes its way inside, replicating sit ups and verbal exercises.

I get off. Not off of him, but come in his mouth, wiggling above him as I hold my ass and surface securely in place on top of him.

Lost in lust, I roll above him and fall flat on the bed. Dante rises from the floor and stands above me upside down.

"You sure you got it all out?" he asks, wiping the evidence from the lower part of his face.

"What do you think?" I close my eyes and exhale.

The buckle from his belt clicks. "I think you want more."

I open my eyes, admiring how pretty his dick looks upside down, poking out like a batter at base.

"If you have a condom in your wallet, why not?" I give in.

The hope in his eyes returns to the look on his face from earlier in the day. He's been granted a pity fuck, and he's excited.

Like a child, Dante takes off all of his clothing. He climbs on top of me, rubbing his covered cock against my stubborn entrance. I suffer through the snagging of the condom, the rhythm-less strokes, and the groaning of a clueless amateur.

When he comes, he lies on top of me, praising how good I feel, and expresses his gratitude. I wriggle from beneath him, take a ho bath in the sink, then order him to get dressed.

Stalling, he reaches for the remote. "Would it be crazy for us to get back together for the summer?"

I throw his shirt on top of his head. "Yes. Get dressed."

"What's the rush? Let's chill here all night. Just you and me."

"Un uh. I have family in town. Hurry up." His pants land across his legs.

He hops up and pulls his shirt over his head. "You wanna come over tomorrow? I'll have the house to my-self for a few hours."

"Again, family."

I grab my purse and lead us through the lobby of the hotel. Dante walks me to my car, and lingers longer than I need him to.

"Call me when your family leaves town." He poses for a kiss.

"I will…And tell your mother hello for me."

I speed off and return home, bombarded with questions of my whereabouts, and the big green and white gift in my hand.

"I just came from hanging with Dante," I say, then quickly add a lie to my story. "We exchanged graduation gifts. He says hello by the way."

Nineteen

Fucking Dante after graduation was enough to make me swear off men for a while. He was just a boy who couldn't fill the shoes of a man who made me wet thousands of miles away by simply talking about sex. Mr. Edge Beaumont.

Edge was who my body wanted. The beautiful stranger my body needed. The image of lust in my dreams igniting a yearning within me I desperately wanted to explore. And I had to have him.

The summer was hot as fire, and so were my erogenous zones I punished with lack of attention from a lousy lay, and the adoration of my fingers at play.

Backed up and filled with excitement, I spent my nineteenth birthday saying goodbye to Lily and my parents, and headed to New York for school. I had no proof my sexual frustration added the necessary mojo required to maintain First Chair at college, but when it was time for my audition, I pressed my violin below my chin, and strummed it with my bow the way I wanted Edge to strum my unused instrument, earning the First Chair of my university's orchestra as a freshman.

CHAPTER THREE

SECONDS

$\mathcal{I}$ share my good news about the honor of First Chair with Edge. He surprises me the following weekend, similar to the way he did for my graduation, but this time I follow his instructions to a five star hotel on the upper east side of Manhattan.

Traveling beneath the tall buildings keeps my attention during the taxi ride below a black skyline filled with lights of a city I had yet to explore. The loudness of the hustle and bustle in the streets, horns blowing, and obscenities shouting between drivers holding up traffic entertains me as I ready myself to be stripped out of this smoky-colored, spaghetti strapped dress, and spread across a hotel bed finally feeling the magic I know Edge will deliver.

I strut inside the lobby, exposing my shoulders in the heat of the New York City night. A bellman waves at me through the thick glass doors, and points towards the front desk.

I exhale deep after the clerk greets me. "Reservation for Natalia Sutton."

He hands me a single red rose and calls a bellhop walking by over to the desk. "Please escort Ms. Sutton to the private dining area."

He takes my arm. "Right this way, Miss."

Dashing and debonair, Edge sits at a table covered with white cloth, and a candle in the center below a glass cylinder shade. The smile on his face sends a chill down my spine. I hold on to the bellhop's arm tighter, securing myself from an embarrassing fall in stilettos adding four inches to my five foot three height.

Edge stands up from the table and pulls out my chair. I shiver when my hand falls into his. He kisses the back of it, then lowers me down with ease before sliding my chair forward. When he sits in the seat across from me, his gray eyes share the reflection of the fire flickering from the candle in the center of the table. I grin because that fire doesn't compare to the heat burning between my thighs.

"I wasn't expecting you," I say, unable to hide the happiness in my voice.

"There was a meeting this morning a few blocks from here. I could have phoned in, but I chose to attend in person—so I could see you. Your picture in my phone has lost its magic." He smiles. "I needed to see you in person."

"Very sweet of you to drop by. How long are you in town for?"

"Let's not start the evening off bitter. I'm here to celebrate all of your achievements since we last saw each other."

A waiter clears his throat and places a gold box in front of me. He and Edge share a nod, then his eyes shift back to me.

"I couldn't tell if you liked your graduation present, so here's another one."

"I love the investments you bought me. One has tripled in profit. Why wouldn't I like that?"

"Well, I wasn't sure, so open this one."

A tennis bracelet with a pear shaped diamond in the middle sparkles in the box. Edge reaches over and lifts the bracelet, then hooks it around my wrist. My arm turns stiff by his touch. My breath skips every second his finger brushes against my skin.

His hand slides down the side of mine and our fingers intertwine. I pose for him, holding my wrist above the candle for him to see.

"Does that mean you like it?"

"I love it. And the financial education you've given me."

He smiles. "Shall we order?"

"Here, or room service?"

Edge sighs. "Natalia."

"Yes?" My nipples harden through the silk.

"I haven't seen you for…"

"Ten months, roughly," I interrupt.

"Let's order and enjoy the evening. I still have to give you your birthday present."

'I hope it's a belated birthday ass waxing.'

"Sorry. I'm still a little shocked to see you in the flesh. It's been so long I began to think I made you up in my mind."

He grabs my hand. "I'm very much real."

Like a gentleman, Edge asks what I want from the menu and orders for me. We discuss his travels over the past few months, how I'm adjusting to the Big Apple, and what stocks to keep an eye on. Before dinner is served, the waiter returns with a second box.

"This one is because I missed your birthday."

I break open the seal of the envelope. "One ticket to the opera?"

"Should there be two?"

"Yes."

"For who?"

"You."

"My sweet girl, I bought you a ticket because everyone should experience the opera alone."

"Have you?"

"I have, and that is why I recommend it. When you are alone you don't have to worry about how the person you're with is feeling, or enjoying it. It's just you all alone, bonding with the story through the emotional range of the performers."

I stare at him with a million more questions to ask. He stares back at me, studying my reaction to the gift and his explanation.

"Are you trying to refine me further than I already am, or open me up to the things you like?"

"Does that mean you don't like this gift?"

"I do like it, and I'll use this ticket. I just wish you were going with me, but I'll take your advice, and report back on my experience."

"That's all I ask of you."

"I do worry you are ashamed of me?"

"Only a stupid man would be ashamed of you. You're gifted, graceful, gorgeous, and soon—mine."

A rush of blood rises to my cheeks. As they flourish and turn pink, the pink between my legs warm with fever and lubes my panties from his choice of words. The torture of being near him and not on him, smelling his cologne, looking into his eyes, and remembering the first time mine caught the attention of his sends a spiraling twist into my stomach.

The soft tune of *Claire de Lune* plays in the background. I hum to its melody, and Edge gazes into my eyes as he reaches for my hand.

"Did I tell you I love this song?" he asks, sweeping his fingers between mine.

"No, you didn't. It's my favorite song played on the piano. I love that version better than on my violin."

"You see that." Edge squeezes my hand. "We just found something else we share in common."

"What was the first?"

"Each other."

I play it coy at dinner, eating small bites from one fourth of my plate though I'm starving. Edge orders the waiter to dispose of my leftovers and places the same entrée as takeout.

My blood begins to boil at the words "to go." A clear indication we aren't spending the night together in a deluxe room upstairs.

I shy away from asking him a second time if we are finally going to fuck, and sit quietly at the table while he reaches into his wallet to settle the check.

While I stew, the waiter places my final gift of the evening in front of me.

Edge adjusts his jacket. "This is for maintaining, First Chair."

I unwrap the gold box and sigh. "I don't get it."

"Being away at school is tough. You have to budget, struggle, suffer, and do without at times."

My brows curve. "How would you know? You have a privileged background."

"I *had* a privileged background. When I decided to stay in Europe, I had the support of my father for a few months. He took care of my tuition, but nothing else. Food, room and board, partying, and supplies fell on me. This chum who had everything given to him was lost when he was forced to face the real world. I don't want that for you. I want you to have everything."

"But what I want is you."

"And you have me."

"What I have is access to your money." I tap the black card with my finger.

"Do with it as you want. There is no limit."

I slide the card in front of him. "I can't…"

"I won't take no for an answer."

"Why don't we have a room upstairs?" I pinch my leg for blurting that question.

He ignores me.

The waiter returns with my order in a black and white bag with aluminum foil shaped in the form of a duck peeking over the top.

"That's how you know you've just enjoyed a fine dining experience, I suppose." I smile at the waiter.

"We hope you've enjoyed your visit." The waiter bows after Edge slips him two one hundred dollar bills.

"I've ordered a car to take you home." He states like he's ending a business meeting with a seriousness in his tone, and a quick glance in my direction.

I hold in a huff and play his game. "Thank you."

We stand in front of the hotel until the car pulls around in the loading zone. Edge opens my door and sits me in the backseat, hovering over me as he reaches for the seat belt. The heat between us melts the remaining lipstick on my lips. *Click.* The latch fastens, and I tremble.

Our eyes meet and my lips part. I'm thirsty for him and he knows it. He's caving fast in abandoning his hunger for me as well. I feel it as he looks at me. So close. So damn close.

He kisses me, then pulls back. Staring into my eyes, his lips press shut while his fingers lift the hem of my dress, just enough for him to slide his hands up past my thighs to the center of my panties.

The shock of how drenched I am hiccups whatever is on the tip of his tongue. A gentle flick of the finger to my outer layer stuns me. Excites me. Dampens me.

I lose my breath and sit still in my drip. I might as well be lying motionless on a gurney because someone is going to have to push me to my destination. I'm frozen, taken aback at the slyness of his motives, yet the scandal of his actions touching me inconspicuously in the public arouses me to no end.

Withholding my breath as the flicks stop, the scent of his after shave teases my nostrils as he holds my gaze. The notes of his cologne invite me to draw him close and take what I want. The power of his eyes weaken me.

I'm unsure if he or I blink as his finger moves my panties to the side, then slides inside my hole. A second finger enters, both pressing upward to the back of my clit. My cream lubes his fingers and I shudder, panting quietly into Edge's mouth.

I grab onto his jacket and exhale. He withdraws his fingers, then kisses me softly one last time.

"Call me when you get home," he says, licks my slick from his fingers and closes the door.

My racing heart nearly stops as I cover my throbbing womb with the takeout bag, and watch him hail for a taxi until my car merges into traffic.

My legs jitter as I smile to myself during the drive home, squeezing my thighs together, high from the in-stant gratification, and the dangerous spontaneity of public affection whilst I'm pissed of the abrupt ending.

I arrive home, and replay the night in my head in a daze on my couch, and make a promise to myself.

'Don't ever call him again.'

The Mindfuck

Since his manly fingers protruded between my folds in the back of a chauffeured car in the big city, the yearning for Edge to touch me increased tenfold. It was a mindfuck I was incapable of handling, leaving me with sensations of wet, erotic visions of him haunting my dreams.

I knew this man wanted me. And he knew he wanted me, too. But for the life of me, I couldn't understand how a man like him was disciplined to fight the dirty desires he and I were destined to share.

His restraint fucked with my psyche, and he fucked with my heart, as well as fucked with my mind—and it became too much.

In turn, I never used the black card he gifted me. I was determined to show him I could manage without his charity, especially since he showed great discipline not to fuck me before I graduated, or turned twenty. But it was his loss. I was over him and under someone else. And he had himself to blame for never knowing what we could have been.

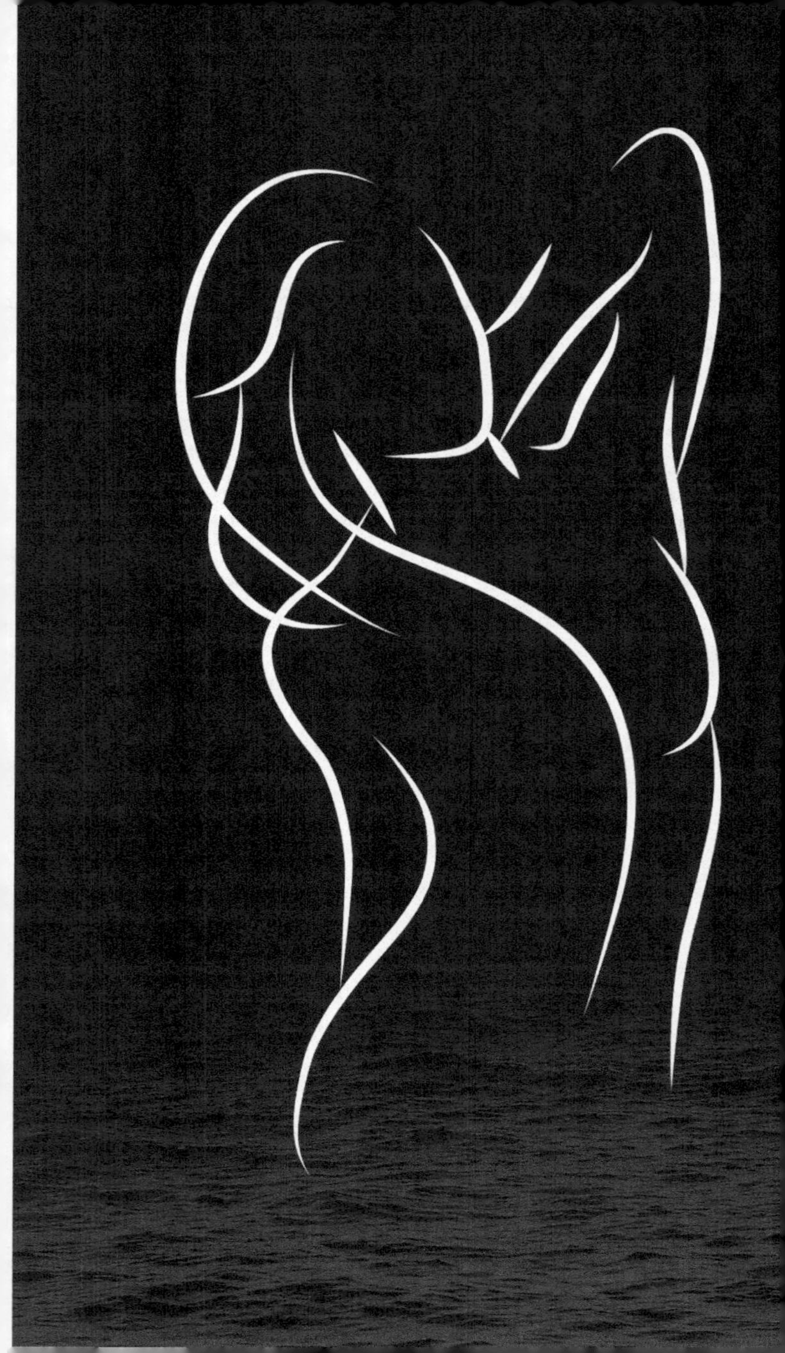

CHAPTER FOUR

THE OPERA

While sitting in the third row of a half empty auditorium, a clean shaven, tawny theatre patron taps me on the back of my shoulder.

"How are you enjoying the show?" he asks.

I twist my hand side to side and pucker my lips.

He leans forward a second time and whispers, "It's not five stars as the reviews suggest."

I nod and smirk at his baby face.

"I play the trumpet," he adds.

"Nice," I whisper, and give him a thumbs up.

"I'd love to pick your brain afterwards." He raises his brows with a goofy smile across his lips.

I shrug my shoulders and return my focus to the kneeling woman singing in soprano about her hardships onstage. After the show, the talkative fellow appears at my side as I type, then erase a text to Edge.

"I'm taking a chance here. I contemplated if I should escort you out of the theatre, or play it cool from across the room and hope our eyes would meet, *or* take one final glance of you and watch you walk away, knowing I would regret it if I never saw you again."

"So what did you decide?" I say, tossing my phone in my purse. I stare at him with a resting bitch face for about five seconds, then snicker at his throat gulping on his pride. His mouth parts slightly, and a light humming sound travels from his throat. I smile. "I'm kidding."

He exhales. "You really had me going. You must be an actress. I believed I really fucked up coming over here."

We both laugh.

"I'm Toran, and you are?"

"Nat."

"I must confess, I tried option two. I stood over there waiting for you to look up, and when you didn't I panicked and convinced myself to come over here and ask if you wanted to grab a coffee or drink sometime?"

"I'm free tonight."

Toran's brown eyes light up. "Shall we?"

We skip two crowded bars and find a cozy coffee shop a few blocks away from the theatre.

"Was I right about the opera?" he asks.

"Maybe."

"I give it three stars," he adds.

"What didn't you like about it?"

"The music. But mostly the length."

I fixate on the lint in his sandy brown hair. "What about the story?"

"It was cool." He nods. "I guess all operas are more drama than anything else, so I'd give that part a five." He puckers his lips then says, "I saw you wipe away a tear before I could hand you my handkerchief at the end."

"I found it highly emotional. I felt all of the lead singer's pain."

Toran drops his head. "Well now I want to change my rating." He looks up at me and smiles. "I give it four stars."

We learn we share a love of music and connect as students of the arts. We talk until the owners begin wiping tables and sweeping the floors around us, and walk out just before they turn off the lights.

"I'd like to see you again." Toran pulls out his phone.

I do the same and scowl that I have zero missed calls or messages.

He stammers. "I'm going to be forward here, and ask that you call me so I can save your number in my phone."

I chuckle at the shakiness in his voice. "Forward, you say." I call him and do a little dance to his ringtone. "How's that?"

"Perfect." He smiles, then hails me a cab.

ONE NIGHT of coffee turns into a second invitation days later to meet his friends during a night of bowling. Talk of an upcoming party circles the room, and Toran invites me to an annual costume Greek Mythology party, but not as a friend–as his date.

He makes an exemplary untanned Zeus with his fake beard hanging from his face by a string. I arrive as Aphrodite with an ivory silk sheet draped around one shoulder below my coat, and say the most insatiable line ever when he opens the door.

"Nice staff."

Toran chuckles below his beard and his eyes glimmer at me. "Aphrodite was the perfect choice for you. Please come in."

I curtsy. "Nice place."

"Thanks." He leads me to sofa. "I feel like an idiot. I invited you in, when we are supposed to be on our way. Should we have a drink first?"

I unbutton my coat. "Champagne would be nice, but I'll settle for anything warm. It's freezing outside."

Toran slides over towards me and reaches for my coat. We play tug of war with it, landing in a sweet lip lock that leads us to the floor. My costume becomes undone as we engage in a passionate twenty minute workout before the party.

I redress in the middle of the living room. "Where can I freshen up?"

"Straight down that hall." He points behind me. "FYI, I'm not introducing you as my date tonight."

I look at him with furrowed brows.

"I'm telling everyone you're my girlfriend."

Quickly our courtship blossoms into regular nights of love making in his apartment, and sometimes back-stage in a dark corner after one of our performances. Toran is gentle and meticulous and spontaneous when the mood strikes him, introducing me to sex out in the open.

Instantly, the thrill of public displays of affection in-crease the adrenaline rush of almost getting caught in the act. A boost I find addictive that triggers a memory of Edge.

Toran invites me over to his apartment the week be-fore winter break. He doesn't greet me when I arrive. He holds the door open and gestures for me to come inside. After the door closes behind me, his arms drape around me and his lips brush my neck. Heavy breaths escape his mouth as he unbuttons my coat, letting it fall to the floor.

My sweater ruffles my hair and my bra flings to the wall. Toran lifts me and wraps my legs around his waist, then carries me to the window overlooking the Manhattan skyline.

My nipples peak at the coldness of winter freezing my back through the glass. Then the chill ices my ass as Toran removes my pants and panties for all of New York to see.

His lips are always moist. He takes excellent care of them because of his craft. Lately, he overuses them on me and I adore him for it, cradling his head between my legs, warming my body against the wide, frigid window, blowing into my pussy like his trombone.

My ass squeaks from the condensation and growing heat of pleasure filling my body, weakened by the tongue play of my hornsman, and his methodical hands squeezing my hips, guiding them back and forth to the perfect rhythm between us.

I cry out. "Don't stop."

The rolling of his tongue sputters inside my walls as his full, skilled lips purse into position like I'm the tip of his mouthpiece. Toran's hands firmly press the sides of my waist and snake their way to my nipples.

"Yes," I moan, falling victim to his sprightly need to please me.

The execution of his finger play drives me wild up high in the city, looking down at the cars speed by, and wondering if someone in one of the adjacent buildings is watching me shiver into a euphoric state.

The thought excites me.

"Now," I moan, pulling Toran's gifted lips away from my greedy pussy.

He rises to his feet and looks down at me. "With or

without?" he asks, with a heavier emphasis on the latter.

"Just do it," I say, licking my palm, then wrap it around his cock.

Toran gasps, "Nat, I'm afraid I'm going to fuck you so hard on this glass we might commit suicide."

I grin at him flattering himself. "Put it in before I change my mind."

A trail of my ass smudges the glass, shrieking from the heat of our passion condensed against the cool air on the other side. Toran's wide enough, and long enough dick breaks into me effortlessly.

He grunts. "I knew you'd feel good, but damn, baby. You're so tight and wet, I don't ever want to leave from inside of you."

I hold onto the back of his head and thrust forward as best I can with little room to move as Toran is all over me. Everywhere at once it seems, clobbering my pussy freely and gleefully.

I suddenly worry about the downside of not using protection.

'He's strapped up with no problem these past few months, I'll consider this his reward for obedience and careful attentiveness of my needs. The test better come back negative.'

I sigh, caught in the rapture of feeling his dick naturally. This is my first time slipping up, and ignoring the advice of my mother to never trust a boy in bed. But I'm high above the big city of dreams.

I trust myself and monthly prescription, and continue to experience the best fuck of my life from a sturdy cock drilling me to pieces, flesh on flesh, hard in my sod, after he *mealed* on my field.

The sounds of Toran exerting himself bring me delight. Like an animal, he roars into my bosom—resembling a lion, near tears of victory and exhaustion. I massage his back and clench my pussy tighter around him. His torso jerks and his breathing slows while he squeezes me in his arms.

Still inside me, he carries me over to the bed, refusing to leave my warmth as his semen trickles down my leg.

We laugh.

"I don't know if that's you or me." He pants.

"Probably both." I maneuver him to my side. "You could use a painting, or some artwork in that space." I point above the headboard.

He rolls on his back. "You think?"

"If not a painting, something abstract."

He draws circles above my chest. "I'll get on it. I didn't call you over here to do this by the way."

"What? Listen to me tell you how to spruce up your place?"

"No. I didn't call you over to hook up. But lucky me. I don't ever want to strap up with you again."

"Don't get carried away, Toran."

"You have no idea how exhilarating that was just now. I'm ready to go again."

"I can see that." My brows rise to his standing cock. "Then, why did you invite me over?"

"I wanted to ask you to come home with me for Christmas. But fuck that now. I'd rather stay here and do this with you."

"My parents would kill me if I didn't come home."

"Well, if I come home with you, you think we'll be able to grab some alone time?" He kisses my cheek. "You've just become my addiction, Nat. I don't want to be without you."

"Pump the brakes, love. I need to call and make sure

my father isn't going to go berserk at the mention of me bringing a boy home."

"My parents are fine with me bringing you home to spend the holidays with us."

"You've already asked them?"

He nods. "They were excited."

"So now if I don't show up, I'll look like the asshole."

"I actually have it all mapped out. If you say yes, we'll fly out together. My father has already agreed to loan me his car to drive you to Aurora. It's only two hours away from Milwaukee. This way, we can spend time with both of our families…If you say yes."

The excitement in his voice tickles me. "I'd love to meet your parents. Just let me work out the details with my folks first, and we'll go from there."

He kisses my forehead, then my lips. "I'm so happy you said yes." He rolls back on top of me. "Now, can I make love to you again?"

"I'd rather you fuck my brains out this time."

Toran groans. "I can't wait to show you off at home."

CHAPTER FIVE

PRESENTS & PRESENCE

My mother is delighted I've found someone eager to take me home to meet his parents.

"You should meet them to get a sense of who you're dealing with, and how far you want this relationship to go. He must like you alot to suggest such a thing," she says.

My lips smack. "I wasn't expecting you to be so cool about this."

"You're in college now. Time to start interviewing potential mates, and learn what you like. Plus, this way your father and I get to meet who you're spending time with when he drives you home."

And so, we follow Toran's plan—two days with the Fisks in freezing Cheese Country on a ranch miles wide. They welcome me with a lovely, colorful family experience. Hugs, offers of beverages from espresso, egg nog, and mixed cocktails, and questions are thrown at me from every angle.

Some of his family speak proper English. Others pronounce words with a diluted German accent and

drag out their vowels, while the youth talk with a mix-
ture of the later, slang and pop culture vernacular.

I feel comfortable around the extended Fisk family,
pouring into the ranch in herds on Christmas Eve as a
part of their tradition to feast on pork cooked in countless ways: smoked on different woods, fried, cured,
shredded, and baked.

They question me in subtle ways and I'm careful to
keep my answers short and concise, fearful I'm in the
line of fire to learn my class and status like Dante's
mother. The vast amount of land the family owns and
lives on makes me assume the third degree is to protect
Toran's inheritance of old family money and genera-
tional wealth from a gold digger. I pass with flying
colors.

After dinner, we gather around the seven foot tree
in the living room and open one present each.

"This one is for Natalia." Mrs. Fisk hands me a shiny
green box with a red ribbon.

"I wasn't expecting anything."

"When Toran said he was bringing his girlfriend
home with him, I wanted to make sure you felt welcome. I know what it's like to be left out," she says.

"Don't start, Eve. Leave the past in the past," his father grumbles.

Toran's mom rolls her eyes at Mr. Fisk. "Anyway, I
hope you like it."

All eyes are upon me as I open my present, while my
eyes keep a close watch of the clock on the wall,
counting the minutes until we hit the road, with a constant prayer that the roads remain clear to make it
home for Christmas dinner. Thankfully, I don't have to
fake my reaction at the thoughtful gift from his mother.

"I love it." I smile, pulling a silver bracelet with conjoined music notes from the box.

Toran takes it from my hands and places it around my other wrist. I think of Edge for the first time in weeks as his fingers brush against my skin fastening the latch.

"There's a gift card to the store inside the box also. I wanted to get you this silver ring shaped in the form of a violin, but I didn't know your size, so it's already paid for on the card. You can order it when you're ready."

I lean over and hug Mrs. Fisk. "You have no idea how lovely this is. Thank you so much."

"I'm beginning to fear my mother's gift for you is better than mine," Toran snarks.

"What did you get me?"

"You'll have to wait and see tomorrow morning."

"Am I allowed to kiss him in front of you, Mrs. Fisk?"

"You don't need her permission," Mr. Fisk answers. "We know what it's like to be young and in love."

Love. I hadn't used that word in my young life. I loved things like music, and handbags, and being First Chair, but not a person. I liked men. Loved being in their company, and being wanted by them. I even loved being the object of desire. But I've never loved anyone besides myself and my parents.

With the approval of Mr. and Mrs. Fisk, I kiss Toran. His family snickers and whispers around the room. The young ones make kissing noises from the corner. His parents smile at each other, and share a look I find impossible to read.

After a planned morning of breakfast, gift exchanges, and packing, we head to my neck of the woods and share an impromptu quickie on the side of the road after an hour drive into the trip. The car is warm, and so are Toran's hands diving between my legs to feel the wet heat he texted about relentlessly last night.

"You texted me like a pussy hound these past two days." I breathe out as I straddle him in the passenger seat.

"Between my mother not giving us a moment alone, and the way I assume your father will have us constrained at the hips, I had no choice but to sext you."

"I bet you jizzed in a sock in your old room."

He laughs. "How did you know?"

"Just shut up and take this pussy." I slide down his dick and shiver from a draft of cool air seeping through the windows. "Sock boy."

Hunching him upright with the excitement of a voyeur in the woods, or a car driving by slowly to catch a glimpse of why the car is rocking side to side, gives me the energy to lift my ass with precision against the bone prodding about inside of me.

My rolling hips fuck him at a mid tempo until he fills my cup. Moments later, my panties soak when we hit a bump in the road.

"I hope your parents like me as much as mine like you," Toran mentions as I reach for my bag in the backseat.

"If they saw what you just did to me, they won't." I lift my glued ass from the leather seats and change my panties.

He blushes. "When are you coming back to the city? My flight leaves Milwaukee in three days. That should be enough family time before they drive me insane."

"I will arrive back in a week or so."

Toran steers the wheel with one hand and grabs his cock with the other. "Me without you for a week. That's going to be a hard task."

"I've spoiled you. Guess I need to do something about that," I tease him, then rub his balls while he drives.

"Nat. We may have to pull over one more time before we get to your parent's house."

I move back to my side of the car. "No need. I'll find a way for us to be together before you drive back in the morning."

My father wastes no time taking Toran into his office for the third degree. My bags sit in the car for an hour before they return from the back of the house with grins between them.

Toran catches a breather and steps outside alone with the excuse to bring in my luggage.

My father gives me a quick nod of approval. "Two musicians with good heads on their shoulders. Very impressive young man you've brought home. How did his folks treat you?"

"Like family. His parents bought me this bracelet for Christmas."

My fathers eyes it closely. "Judging from their son, and this thoughtful gift, it comforts me that you've chosen well for yourself. Maybe your mother is right. I don't have to worry about you. You're talented, wise, and all grown up." He hugs me.

My father's comment makes me think of Edge. He has it all wrong about my choices, and a tiny hint of guilt encompasses me.

Toran brings in sloshes of snow with him, and drops the bags to warm his hands with his mouth.

"You two better get washed up for dinner." My father lets go of me and joins my mother in their bedroom.

I rush Toran upstairs with my suitcases, and close my bedroom door. "Do you think you can be quiet?" I whisper.

"What? Now? With your father downstairs? I'm not taking that chance after the talk we just had. In fact, show me to my room before he comes up here."

"Scaredy cat."

"More like I-like-my-balls-cat."

I lead Toran back downstairs. My mother pops out of her room as we hop from the bottom step.

"Which room did you set up for Toran?" I ask.

She waves for us to follow her. "I put fresh towels and linens on the bed in this room."

I snicker. "Why next to Dad's office?"

My mother scowls.

"Did Dad install some sort of spy-cam in here to make sure he has eyes on Toran at all times?" I search the shelves for gadgets.

The scowl on mom's face lifts. "I wouldn't be surprised if he has." She titters. "But in all seriousness, no, I didn't put him in the big room because your father's friend is coming to dinner tonight."

"What friend?" The center of my back stiffens and my fingers tingle.

"The friend who spent Christmas with us last year. Your father says he's come into town with a guest, and thinks he is going to pop the question. The Palmers are coming tonight also."

I turn to Toran. "Make yourself at home and change for dinner, please. I'll be back dressed to impress." I tap on the wall and follow my mother to the front of the house.

"He's cute." My mother chills me with a piercing look. "Your father seems to like him. So do you."

"That makes two out of three." I stare back at her.

"We'll see. Papa Bear may have the gun, but Mama Bear is still the one you have to watch out for. Run along and get changed for dinner."

I wait to hear noise in the kitchen and scream into my hand at the news.

'Edge is bringing some bitch to my house, on my holiday! The fucking nerve of this man! How am I supposed to look him in the eye like I don't give a damn he's left me dwindling in the wind like a piece of flyaway paper? Fuckin' pussy.'

With a racing heart I barge into Toran's room. He covers his bare legs and crouches over.

"Just in time," I whisper, then lock the door.

"Stop girl. I mean…I want you, too…but…you know what I mean." He kisses my cheek and squeezes my ass.

My hands rest on his chest. "You scared?"

His eyes grow big. "I wanna get in there, but I'll wait. Stop trying to get me in trouble." He throws on his pants. "Everything okay?"

My lips sputter. "Yeah, everything is fine." I lie, panicked about Edge coming to dinner. "I'm just thinking of a place you and I can be together tonight before you leave me tomorrow."

"I know I can be a hound, but if it doesn't happen, the more explosive it will be when we reunite in the city."

I smooch his lips. "You're a sweetheart. And you look good. I better go get dressed."

The doorbell rings while I'm throwing clothes around my room. I stop breathing and hold my chest. Nothing can prepare me for seeing the man I trained my mind to forget, but my heart chooses to hold onto.

His laugh travels through the vents as he greets my father. I ease my door open and peek around the wall to see his face, and the woman who stole him from me. The man that promised to be mine in a few months when I turn twenty.

Her back is turned to me, and I imagine pulling her brown curly hair up and down the staircase until she promises to get out of my house. Her ass is nice, I give her credit for that, and her shoes have red paint on the bottom—courtesy of Edge I'm sure.

I quietly return to my room and 86 the Christmas sweater dress. Scrolling through the outfits I left hanging in my closet, I change into a red mini dress with cutouts on the shoulder, slip on my leather thigh high boots, and free my hair from the pulled back ponytail.

"Natalia! We're waiting for you, Dear!" my mother calls.

I hold onto the wooden banister as I work my way down the stairs and take a long, deep breath before stepping into the dining room.

"Sorry to keep you all waiting. Happy Holidays." I wave, avoiding eye contact with Edge.

"Natalia!" Lily hops up from her chair and hugs me. "We have to get a moment alone. Your boyfriend is a catch," she whispers in my ear.

"Yes, we do," I whisper back.

Toran interrupts, "Babe, what a small world. Your

parents know my uncle." He points to Edge. "This is my mother's brother. Uncle Living Life on the Edge."

I turn and meet Edge's eyes shining like silver ornaments hanging from the tree.

'Uncle? You have got to be fucking kidding me.'

"Really? It is a small world," I say, then whisper to Lily. "We have a lot to fucking talk about."

I sit in the middle of Lily and Toran, directly across from Edge. The lust I feel for him still stands, and the tiny ounce of *'I am pissed you brought a woman to my house'* hides on my face.

He glances at me quickly, then drops his fork. He scoots back from the table and leans down to pick it up. I open my legs and stick my middle finger at him. Then, I talk over Lily to address her parents.

My mother stands at the end of the table next to my father. She taps the stem of her glass and clears her throat.

"As you can see from the smile on my face, this has been a glorious Christmas. Our daughters Natalia and Lily left us at the end of summer, and have safely returned home to us for the holidays. We are happy to celebrate today with our guests, and friends of many years, and welcome to our new guests, Toran and Calliope. Cheers to a very happy holiday."

"Cheers!" Everyone lifts their glasses.

"Let's eat." Dad pats my mother's seat.

As the casserole dishes are passed around the table, I wonder why this woman's mother named her Calliope, and how she managed to weave her way back into Edge's life. She catches me glaring at the massive diamond on her engagement finger.

"Natalia, your mother says you have been the First Chair in the orchestra for several years. I think she was being modest. You must be a child prodigy of some sort."

'This bitch just called me a child.'

I force a fake smile. "My mother doesn't like to brag about me. She's the sweetest woman in the world. She raised me to be the same in that light, so I won't brag about my achievements. I've just worked really hard to be the best."

"I think you've more than earned to brag from what I hear," she adds.

'Bitch, let it go. I don't want to talk to you.'

I pleasantly smile with my lips pressed tightly bound. "Thank you." I squeeze through my teeth.

"Will you play for us after dinner?"

'Hell no, bitch.'

"Sorry, I stopped entertaining my parents' friends after I finished high school. I'm on a break, so that is what I intend to do. Break free from everything and relax."

My mother side eyes me. "Hopefully, she'll change her mind."

"Nephew," Edge interrupts. "How did you meet Sy's daughter?" He looks at me quickly, then back to Toran.

'Sy's daughter? So you can't call my name now? You shitty pussy teasing bastard.'

I breathe through the anger rising in my chest.

"Funny story." Toran chortles. "Mom's group canceled their trip to New York, and she was beside herself that the tickets she paid for the opera would go to waste. She begged me to pick them up at the Will-Call office. So, I stood out front, offering the tickets to people walking by, then I saw Natalia go inside. When I failed to give away the tickets, I used one of them and went in myself."

"You never told me this." I tug on his arm.

"We got on so well I didn't think I needed to tell the woman sitting three rows from the front I was there on a technicality, or using his mother's tickets." He chuckles. "I would have struck out before coming up to bat if I had told you that." Toran looks at my Father. "Am I right, Mr. Sutton?"

My dad laughs. "He's right dear. You wouldn't have given him a second glance."

"She never gave me the first glance. She was into this opera. Like studying it for an exam or something."

"Is that right?" Edge peers at me.

Toran's hand sweeps my back. "Yes, like way into it. And her tickets were way better than mine, so I had to bribe the usher twenty bucks to let me sit in her section."

"How did you get such good tickets, Natalia?" My mother asks.

My eyes bug and I blurt out, "A cellist got sick and offered them to me." I turn back to Toran. "Finish telling them, Honey."

"I sparked some small talk, she brushed me off, then I took a chance and asked her out for coffee. Now here we are, a match made in Heaven, celebrating our first Christmas together." He leans in to kiss me, but stops and looks at my father.

My father gives him the okay. Toran shifts his aim from my lips to my cheek. I giggle at his inferiority to my dad and smush his lips, brushing his nose with mine.

"My experience at college has been the complete opposite." Lily gulps her champagne. "Maybe I should transfer to a school in New York."

"If you do, we can be roommates."

"Don't tempt me," says Lily. "Let's talk more about it after we eat."

Edge uses Toran's ignorance of our illicit affair to pry on what I have been up to. Every question he asks at dinner is calculated, propelling Toran to share more than he needs to. And when he spills I have been to the penthouse apartment, Edge humors me as he fails to hide his fury behind a fake smile.

'That's right. This pussy's been popping for three months.'

"Edge, leave the boy alone." Calliope looks at Toran and mouths, "I'm sorry," under her breath.

"How about you, Unc? How did you meet Ms. Calliope?"

'No one wants to hear that shit!'

Calliope clings to Edge's arm and rests her head on his shoulder. "You want to tell them, or should I?"

"Go ahead." Edge folds his hands.

"We're engaged." Her diamond sparkles as she says the words.

"I knew he was going to propose," my father blurts.

My mother raises her glass. "Congratulations."

Dad and Mr. Palmer reach across the table and shake Edge's hand. I applaud the happy couple as Calliope's rock is examined by Lily, then share a moment with Edge as he looks past her and at me.

"It's about time you stopped living on the edge." Toran says to his uncle. "Get it."

Edge calls him over. "Come, my boy. Give your uncle a hug."

I take a deep breath and shake off the look of uncertainty Edge shares with me, then sneak away with Lily while the older ones talk about the impending wedding.

"Did you see that rock on her hand?" Lily rants, following me upstairs.

"I saw it." I huff.

"Lucky lady. If a man that fine asked me to marry him, I'd say yes in a heartbeat."

"No you wouldn't. Now tell me why State isn't working out for you."

"Remember when you said I would have a harem of lovers at school?"

"Yeah."

"Well, that kind of came true."

"I was only joking, Lily. What the fuck have you done?"

"I can't shake three of them. And they want to fuck all the time. I'm going to need an extra set of lips down there if I can't get rid of at least one of them."

"How many have there been?" I laugh.

Lily counts her fingers aloud as she names her lovers. "Five. But I only want to keep two. I thought I could handle three, but there's only so many hours in a day, and I have classes, and work study." She shrugs. "One of the clingers flew to Chicago, caught the bus, and is held up in a hotel in town. I can't shake him for shit."

"Maybe if you stand him up, he'll get the picture."

She whines. "Maybe…maybe not. Who am I kidding? That's not going to happen."

"Why not?"

"After watching you get loved on, I'm most definitely going to the hotel to get plucked. I need advice on how to get rid of him afterwards."

I throw a pillow at her. "You're the problem, Lily. Get out of my room."

Toran meets us at the foot of the stairwell. Lily giggles as she walks past him, turns around, and pokes her tongue against the inside of her cheek. I shake my head and fan off her obscenity.

"I haven't given you your present." Toran surprises me with a rectangular box hiding behind his back. "Open it."

I untie the box and smile.

"I haven't been able to capture the look in your eyes when I first saw you. I thought if I took you to see more theatre shows, I'd see that spark once again."

"I love your mother's bracelet, but this is so thoughtful and sweet. I love it." I stand on my toes to kiss him. "This is way better than the blazer I got you."

Toran laughs. "So it's a blazer in that huge box. I guessed it was a painting. You know—for the space on the wall."

I lower my head. "I'm sorry I spoiled it."

"Toran," Edge interrupts, "They're about to serve dessert."

'He's purposely refusing to call my name.'

Toran kisses me. My eyes roam over to Edge staring at us with flared nostrils and loathsome eyes.

"Come on." Toran takes my hand. "Let's see what the old folks are talking about now."

A few hours of dancing, gossiping, secret stares, and munching on pies, cakes, and leftovers takes us into midnight. The Palmers depart, and our guests retire for the evening.

I unlock my desk drawer and read my journal entries from last Christmas. My words come alive on the page, forcing me to feel the angst between me and Edge.

Every emotion I felt last Christmas is still present, with a few new sentiments to add. This time, I am not lonely or alone, but in shock, and hurt the man with the power to make me feel like a woman with something as simple as a look, brought a woman into my home when he knows he wants to fuck me, and owes me as much.

The situation calls for ice cream. Cold Brew Cookie Dough on a sugar cone is needed to settle me down on this restless night.

I throw on my robe and slip into the kitchen to search through the many flavors, but it's as if my likes have been forgotten and replaced with horrid, dairy free cartons since I no longer live here.

I look out the kitchen window. The roads are too icy to drive to the market, and the only gas station open at this hour is a twenty minute walk away. I settle for a spoonful of vanilla, eating it directly from the box.

Dissatisfied, I shove the pint back into the freezer and make my way upstairs to call it a night. Edge stands in the entrance of the bathroom in the hallway. I pause with my foot on the first step of the stairwell and give into his gaze.

We stare at each other for countless seconds. I wish I could read his thoughts to understand why the fuck he would return here for the holidays after we haven't spoken for months. Why he thinks it's okay to bring *Coca-Cola* to my house and parade her around in my face? And now stare at me with those gray eyes of his, twitching his lips like he wants to lay them on me, and taste what he has put off for too long. Or at least that is what I want him to do with them. Even after all that has been done.

A noise from down the hall breaks our gaze. I gasp and slowly pace back to my room and scream into my pillow, eventually falling asleep with it held tightly in my arms.

By midafternoon the roads are salted and shoveled. Toran takes off while I hide in my room for hours, waiting for the engaged couple to leave.

"Natalia!" my father calls. "Put on your coat! We have something we want to show you!"

I meet the adults outside on the sidewalk. Like one big happy family, the five of us pile into my father's SUV. The pit of the ride is suffering in the back seat with Calliope and my mother looking at wedding dresses on her phone. The peak is sharing smiles with Edge in the side rearview mirror along the drive.

My father pulls into the housing development he calls his pride and glory. "Everyone, this is the last house my firm built in this subdivision. Pera and I are thinking of selling our home and buying this one." He looks at my mother with a huge smile on his face.

"What? Why?" I ask.

"Come inside. You'll see why."

The upgrade of subway tile backdrops, finished ceilings, frog room, enclosed pool, and open floor space are pretty and new, but this isn't home.

I hang back in the room my mother says will be mine if they chose to buy. It is double the size of my current room, and big enough to be a studio apartment in New York.

As I pace the hardwood floors and ogle the huge closet space, Calliope and my mother step outside to talk about gardens and patio spaces.

"With a room like this, I know you'll always come home," says my father as his phone rings. "Excuse me. I need to take this." His footsteps fade on his way out of the house.

"We find ourselves alone in your room—again.

Wonder what that means?" Edge questions, brushing his hands against mine.

"I wish I knew the answer to that." I stare at my mother and his fiancé through the window walking the grounds below.

"So you've been to the apartment?" His voice deepens, picking me for information.

"A few times."

"And you never wondered how Toran was able to live a high-profile life?"

"I don't care about that. My family isn't broke. It's not like I need anything from him. Or you?" I move from his side.

"Why haven't you used the card I gave you?"

I huff. "Stop toying with me Edge. You act like you want me, you give me nice gifts, set a timeline for when we can be together, and you tease me when you see me. Now you suddenly have a fiancé when that time is near. What game are you playing?"

A croak sound bellows in his throat. "I didn't plan on seeing Calliope again. We ran into each other by chance, and lonely people do what lonely people do. She and I kind of—I don't know how else to say it. Once we started up again, we didn't stop this time."

"But why did you bring her here?"

"That wasn't by design. I had plans to come here with the hopes of seeing you, but Sy said you were spending the holidays with a friend. I didn't know you were going to be in town until he called to confirm I was coming to dinner because your mother needed a headcount. As for Calliope, she and I weren't supposed to see each other until New Year's Eve. She surprised me by flying in a few days early. I wouldn't have brought her here had I known your plans changed."

"So this is you in love?" I smirk.

He sighs. "Don't do that."

I step back in his face. "You won't hurt my feelings. As you can see, I have my own thing going on. Things have changed in a year, haven't they?"

Edge grunts. "I guess they have."

"It's funny. Last Christmas I was getting finger banged by you. And this Christmas I was sitting on your nephew's face."

Edge pulls me close. "You shut your mouth. You'll end it with him when I tell you to."

"I will do no such thing. Aren't you happy with *Kalamazoo?*"

Edge smirks. "You're jealous."

"So are you." I pull away from him. "Don't forget to hide my panties before your wife finds them."

I join my mother and the soon to be Mrs. Beaumont outside. Edge stands in my would-be bedroom looking down at us from the window. When the grown women aren't looking, I stare back at him, imagining he is fucking me against that very window sill the way his nephew fucked me in his apartment above the city skyline.

My walls pulsate in the cold breeze blowing the scent of chocolate past my nose. My mind travels to an alternate reality where we are alone in this house, and my white nightgown lifts above my breasts as he strokes me ferociously against the wide frame, leaving a new ass print on the glass with every thrust.

He feeds me chocolate every time I come on his cock, and I lick his fingers clean.

"Natalia, what are you staring at?" My mother pulls on the arm of my coat.

I snap out of the vision and notice Edge is gone.

"Nothing," I lie. "I was just wondering if I'll like that room better than the one I've known my whole life."

"Well, we haven't decided as of yet. But either way, you'll have a place to call home. Come on. Let's get you warmed up. Your nose is turning red."

On the drive home, I ask my father to stop by the store to pick up my flavor of ice cream. As I stand in the checkout line, I read a headline on one of the rag mags about some celebrity couple caught in a love triangle scandal of father and son.

I laugh to myself, guilty I was currently fucking a musician with thoughts of fucking his uncle the magician. Edge, the master of disappearing acts with mind tricks, reeling me in and keeping me at bay, toying with my affections to want him more and more with every breath like an addiction. And I am just that. Addicted.

Spring washed away my affair with Toran. I couldn't bring myself to utter that four letter word I'd never used, even though he was worthy, and he couldn't understand my reluctance to dive into a full-fledged relationship.

He broke it off with me, and denied my request to continue on as friends with benefits. And I was blindsided.

We ended on sour terms, which was on brand for the change of season, as April brought endless showers, and May didn't bring any flowers—from anyone.

Freshman year ended, and I went home to a new house in Aurora, bored for the first few weeks, until Lily and I followed a group of super rich kids she met at State backpacking across Europe.

Out of state. Out of time. Out of the country for a good time.

CHAPTER SIX

THE ROARING TWENTIES

Turning twenty with a group of high, drunk, privileged students isn't how I thought I'd celebrate leaving my teen years behind. Beneath an open, star-filled sky, orange sunset, and bonfire in the middle of a field in Lithuania during the Summer Solstice Celebration, I inhale the European air and bond with nature amongst strangers.

Giving into the peacefulness flowing freely on the grounds, I follow the rituals of the locals and hunt for fern flowers–wandering like a hippie in search of a legendary fern blossom said to give its chosen finder mysterious powers, and enduring pleasure. I haven't known pleasure since my break-up with Toran, so I hunt with intensity for this magical blossom a part of me believes in, with hopes the legend is true, and it will grant me the pleasure I have been dreaming of for nearly two years.

Against my wishes, Lily wanders from my side. I find myself turned around in the woods surrounded by distant chatter and eerie laughter of the other hunters in the darkness falsely claiming they've stumbled across the fern.

I turn to follow their voices, and my heart jumps from my body. White eyes glow at me from behind leaves near an old tree. My feet fail to run as I study the silhouette walking towards me. My mouth opens to call for help, but it shuts as a young man stands inches away from me.

"I saw you with your friends during the ceremony," he says. "Your group stands out in this crowd, and you stand out from them like the color red on a sepia canvas."

My breath hitches, and my heart feels like it has stopped beating, as strips of moonlight creep between the trees, highlighting his hazel eyes looking deep into mine.

"Never heard that one before. Who are you?" I ask him.

"I won't tell you my name. And I won't ask yours."

I narrow my eyes at him. "Why not?"

"There's no need. We won't ever see each other again after tonight."

The hairs on my arm cool above the goosebumps prickling from my skin. "And you know this, how?"

His face is blank and he doesn't answer.

"I'm going to join my friends now. Nice meeting you," I say, but my feet fail to move.

"I heard one of your friends say it's your birthday."

He grabs my hand and pulls my chest next to his. We share a peck on the lips. A closed mouth kiss that feels surreal with time standing still.

"I wanted to kiss you the moment I laid eyes on you," he says.

"And now that you have, what do you think?"

I wait to be released from his hold.

"I think I was wise to not miss the opportunity. Happy birthday."

I'm speechless for the first time in years. My cheeks turn a flaming hot pink. My legs are locked and still like a broken clock.

"Thank you." I finally manage to say to him.

He smiles. "You won't find the fern, but continue having fun looking for it. I'll remember this as the moment I kissed the prettiest girl I ever laid eyes on."

"And I, as the night I let a strange boy kiss me and didn't get his name."

The stranger lets go of me and disappears into the woods. I wipe his kiss from my mouth and trail the laughter of hunters close by, following them back to the bonfire.

I sit alone with my knees to my chest, scouring the playful, lively crowd for the boy from the woods. I see happy, painted faces, flower crowns, and garlands all around me, but not him.

The scent of healing herbs and wildflowers envelope me and I stop searching for him in the horde. He said we would never see each other again, and it dawns on me he was the magical fern I was searching for.

Lily and the group resurface.

"You having fun?" she asks.

I nod, contemplating if I should tell her about my creepy, magical encounter in the woods. I decide against it, embracing the strangeness of it with the sweet.

The burning fire brings in the dawn of the next morning. I feel a difference blossoming inside of me from my Summer Solstice kiss, igniting a change I can't put into words as my sophomore year is upon me.

I'm one year older, one year wiser, and grateful the boy in the woods reminded me of the phrase, *"Not all those who wander are lost."*

'Twenty seems promising.'

CHAPTER SEVEN

TWO NIGHTS BEFORE CHRISTMAS

Twirling winds drop mounds of snow in the city, crippling it into darkness. Layered in wool sweaters and scarves, I find warmth in the kitchen while I bake a boxed lasagna.

The notification bell on my phone chimes.

*All flights flying out of New York
have been delayed until further notice.*

I sigh.

'There goes my trip home in the morning.'

My mother calls me in a panic. I assure her I will try everything to make it home, even if it's late Christmas night.

As we hang up, the power blinks, then fully fails.

A second notification appears on my phone.

*Citywide blackout.
We are working to restore power.*

I become nervous sitting in the dark. Quickly, any

gratitude I have leaves me as my mind complains of not having an apartment with a fireplace. I grab the extra blankets from the closet and eat the lasagna that's cooling faster than I would like.

I check to see if train tickets are available to escape the city in the morning, and panic further as their website reads, *Temporarily Unavailable*.

I snuggle under a blanket, and stare at the ceiling with catastrophic intruding thoughts building fear in my mind.

A text appears on my phone that reads.

How are you?

My heart flutters and my brows raise. I read the message at least a dozen times, then turn my phone face down.

The heat begins to fade in my apartment and I tremble. I throw a second blanket on top of the first with shaky hands, still indecisive if *and* how to respond to the text.

My phone buzzes again.

I hear you are still in the city. How are you making it in the dark?

I'm making good use of my blankets.

I'm stuck here, too. But I have a fire going and plenty of wood. Can I come pick you up?

How? The roads are bad and the city is shut down.

Be there in thirty minutes.

I use the last of my hot water to freshen up before throwing on another layer of wool, sweater socks, and fur lined boots. I pack an overnight bag of flannel pajamas and underclothes. Then, I wait in silence for him to arrive.

He knocks and I shiver. More than I have from the cold. I don't want to appear too eager to see him, so I count to ten before answering the door. When I open it, he grins at me above a black scarf tucked inside the collar of a charcoal gray military wool coat covered in snowflakes.

"Natalia." Edge smiles at me. "You look ravishing, Sweet Girl."

I smile at him with my eyes. "You look the same."

He looks past me into my apartment. "Where's your bag?"

I point to the sofa.

He comes inside and looks around with a smug approval of my place, then drapes my duffel over his shoulder.

"Shall we?" he asks, with his hand in the small of my back.

I unwrap the blankets from my shoulders and throw on my coat. He takes the scarf from my hands and bundles it around my collar. I stare into his grays, and smile to myself below the top layer.

My pace matches his along the walk toward his penthouse. Our eyes catch the other's peeking every block. Our gloves intertwine as we shiver with each step. We attempt small talk, but it's too cold to converse without our scarves covering our mouths, so we walk in silence and speak with our eyes.

His lifts on the outer corners as he smiles below his scarf. "Let's get you inside," he says, opening the door to the building.

He ushers me inside, trailing on my heels as we climb to the top floor. Briefly, I hesitate when he opens the door. The heat of the fireplace lures me inside, and I exhale at its warmth, grateful that my heart's torturer called and rescued me.

Edge places his hands on my shoulders to take my coat. I hide my excitement as the sleeves slowly roll off my arms, and watch him hang it with care on the wooden knob next to the door.

He takes my hand and leads me to the sofa he's turned to face the fire. As my iced bones melt, the layers I'm draped in peel off one by one.

My boots come off. My feet rest on his lap. He rubs them until I close my eyes and my shoulders lie back on top of the arm rest. His hands rise above my ankles. My socks roll past my toes, and I twitch at the feel of his hands caressing my heels. They rise and I freeze at the warmth of his lips gently nibbling on my toes.

I am his without discussion. A year passed us by with zero communication, random gifts in the mail, and minimal words shared between us, but it doesn't matter. One phone call and here I lay as his to conquer and play with. *Finally*.

I squirm as the nibbles turn to sucks on my toes. I'm wet for him. Waiting to be touched in the place I've forbidden to others, but owned by him.

His lips stop short kissing my calves. The lower palm of his hands press firmly against my pussy. I moan as the bone prods forward and retracts, forward again, and rolls around until the saturation filling my panties seeps through to his fingers.

His low vibrato turns me on as he says, "Oh, Sweet Girl. We're going to have so much fun."

He licks his palm and pulls the elastic of my pants down past my hips. His low cut nails claw on my thighs, pressing on my muscles—causing my pussy to throb.

My folds ripple. My back arches, anticipating the curious touch of his fingers. The touch that lit this flame two years ago, spread me open and apply pressure, working their way towards my inner thighs.

He massages an undiscovered erogenous zone that has never been touched. I gasp aloud and spread as wide as the band of my pants will allow.

Drips of my pussy squish as Edge's thumbs rub the dip below the sides of my exterior. I call his name in a low whisper of desire, "Edge," and wind against the sofa while the fire crackles wood, adding to our heat.

"You've come darling," I hear him say.

I'm too far gone to open my eyes from the ingenuity of his intricate finger play, making me come from the flick of a finger, and now a thumb rub.

Whatever else is in store for the evening, I know I won't be in control, and I am okay with that–unless he tortures me and refuses to put his cock inside of me.

I push my pants towards his face with my panties stuck to the seat. Edge strips them from around my feet and throws them to the floor. He tears off his sweater and finally exposes his chest. The weights he lifts form a cut between his chest, and the top of his abdomen.

I signal for him to come to me. He places his tongue on my shin, and licks a wet trail up my thigh. I shudder in formidable delight.

"Look at me," he commands.

My eyes lock with his as he licks my pussy with one

stroke, keeping his tongue pressed on my flesh, trailing it up to the line of my torso between my breasts, and up to my lips.

He kisses me. "Taste it," he orders, drawing my tongue from my mouth. "That's good pussy, isn't it?"

I moan, "Umm hmm."

He drops below me and swirls his tongue around my wetness then returns to my lips. "Taste it again."

Our lips lock, and he moans in my mouth. "I can't wait to swell your sweet cunt, my sweet girl."

I lose it mentally and feel like I'm dreaming. A tingling sensation trills my body from the softness of his tongue dipping between my lips. His kisses, his caress, his hypermasculinity and aggressiveness is unmatched. With an open mouth he inverts and reverses his lips to cuff my folds. I hunch his face, holding his head with both hands, squealing and tightening my pussy muscle with every thrust.

His lips release their clutch. He pulls away for a quick breath of air. "Fuck my face," he whispers, turning to his back, and mounting me on top of his five o'clock shadow.

His hands cradle my inner thighs, and his mouth opens wide. I swing my hips back and forth and pinch my nipples, looking down at half his face reflex from munching on my chocha, quenching his thirst.

One of his hands slides upward and rubs my clit. As my body quakes and my cream covers his tongue, he lifts me up to breathe, rotates my body, then bends my back forward. His tongue takes long strides from my woman hole to my ass hole. I holler of shock, face to face with his trapped dick, fully engorged beneath his trousers.

I gnaw on the zipper, then free it. Taking a deep

breath, I stuff his perfect, beige, shiny, girthy cock in my mouth, winding my asshole against his nose stuck between my ass cheeks.

Edge groans. "Yes, baby. Swallow that dick."

"Ahugh." I gasp for air, sucking him with my jaws drawn in tight.

At my eye level, his balls blossom to the size of tangerines. I suck him hard and fast, becoming heavily aroused watching his thigh muscles grow stiff, and his toes point outward on each foot.

When I slow down my suction and swirl my tongue around the bellend of his cock like an ice cream cone, he calls my name. "Natalia."

I inhale and hold my breath, then glide his head down my throat slowly, rolling my head side to side in a figure eight motion.

Edge wails, "My sweet girl!"

I exhale and choke, breathing through my nose as he jolts and squeezes his legs together.

I come up for air. Edge exhales and relaxes with his head tilted back. I dive back down, and he sighs, massaging my lower spine when his hands aren't spreading my ass like an eagle's wings.

Then, his thumb invades my back door. My pussy gyrates from the unknown source of gratification my experienced lover bestows upon me.

My back weakens as I gag on his cock. Tears trickle from my eyes, but I'm no quitter. I tease his brick hard dick with licks, and kisses, and sucks, and tugs, stroking rings with my thumb and index finger following the lead of my lips going up and down until the scent of chlorine hits my nose.

'No, Mr. Beaumont. You will not rob me of feeling your cock.'

I slide my drenched pussy down his picture-perfect chest. As I lift up, he stops me.

"No. No. No. You will not deny me this," I say, staring into his eyes.

He grins. "Calm down, my eager princess. Are you on something?"

I smile. "Yes. You." I split my pussy open with his dick.

He gasps. "I meant the pill." He adds with a cracked voice rolling his hands around my ass.

"Yes, Edge," I moan. "We're good."

His hands grab my waist as he plunges his dick hard into my pussy. I'm in reverse cowgirl riding the bull of my dreams, enduring the agonizing, painful, pleasure of Edge Beaumont, my silver fox lover.

From my waist to the center of my back, his hands worm up to my head, grabbing a lock of my hair. He tugs on it while my back arches, sticking his thumb back in my ass, and I yowl.

"You're all I dreamed you would be," he grunts, fucking me strong like an ox.

"Am I? Mr. Beaumont?"

"I'm gonna be fucking this tight pussy all night. Get up," he orders with such authority in his voice.

I obey his command and rise to my feet. He stands next to me, wide legged and amplified, lowering me to my knees.

With a gentle slap to my mouth he says. "Open."

I do so with volition.

He sticks his hand in my mouth and holds it still until water produces in my eyes, then rolls his cock against my lips. I stick out my tongue, and he taps the tip of his dick against it while holding the back of my head. *Tap, tap, tap* it smacks on my tongue until he plunges it down the pink trail of my mouth.

"That tastes good, doesn't it, baby?" he mewls with his eyes closed.

But mine are wide open, watching the inverted V on his abs feed his cock and the juice of my pussy down my throat.

"Just like that. Yes. Your mouth was made to suck my cock," he moans, slowing the roll of his hips.

He withdraws and leans down to kiss me with passion, and I am gratified by the tone of his moan. I melt when I open my eyes and look into his, mesmerized by the reflection of the fire burning in the center of his gorgeous grays.

He grins and positions me in a leaning pose slightly backwards, and hovers his cock over me with a small step forward.

"Squeeze them," he says, pinching my nipples.

The sensation of an overdue stretch vibrates from the wing of my back, down to my pussy as I press my breasts together. I'm enamored by the height of him towering me like a giant, and the smell of my pussy layered on his balls as his fingers roll around my nipples.

One hand wraps around my throat. "Open up one more time for me like a good girl."

Talking to me like that makes my pussy throb. I want him back inside of me, saying sweet nothings, and telling me what to do in a raspy, dominating tone. But I do as he says and part my lips.

"Stick that tongue out for me."

I roll it past my bottom lip.

Edge taps his stiff cock against it again, holding his shaft at the base. I see the excitement in his eyes, and admire the control of his pace to not force feed his needy cock where it wants to be.

The pattering sound of it defiling my tongue makes the head of his dick grow bigger.

"Good girl. Now spit on it."

I drool like he asks.

"A little more," he coaches me.

I release a little more spittle. It drips down my chin to my chest, then Edge grabs my throat and hair, and slides his dick between my smushed breasts, fucking himself with the slickness of my saliva between the softness of my pillows.

Staring deep into my eyes as he chokes me and fucks my tits, he croaks, "You're a perfect little minx."

"Does this feel good to you?"

"All of you feels good to me," he mutters.

I stick out my tongue and lick his hole when he pushes through.

"Aah." His shoulders quiver.

"I want you to fuck me some more," I beg.

Edge smacks his cock against my cheek, and quickly gags me with an unexpected maneuver down my throat. I hold my heave.

He whimpers. "You learn quickly, don't you sweet girl."

My body lifts from the floor and he throws me on the sofa, spreading both of my legs to the side and in the air. He rides me hard against the cushions and asks, "Like this? You want me to fuck your tight pussy like this?"

"Yes. Like this," I whine, trapped beneath him, searching for air between the cracks of my thighs pressed to my face.

I shriek under my breath, withstanding his cock disciplining my pussy for begging to be lashed. Edge pounds me like dough, grunting above me with strong strokes, then pulls out of me to stand back. My pussy opens and closes like a drawbridge welcoming a ship through.

"Look at that pretty pussy pulse for me to break it in," he says, then dives back inside.

I hold his head to mine, never wanting this moment to end—holding him close enough to feel his racing heart work to fuck me as he's wanted to since we met—how I've wanted him to since we met.

His rhythm speeds to an unimaginable pace. His voice shrills and his breathing stunts as a sudden warmth bursts inside of me. I hold on to his side, listening to him barely breathe as he comes inside my pussy clenching tight around his jolting dick.

Edge presses the head of his cock to the back of my wall and I hold his penis prisoner. His tight shoulders relax and he exhales a final deep breath before withdrawing his cock.

He slides down and kisses my hole before his drip seeps out, then circles my pussy with his finger around the orifice.

I whimper and tremor, looking up at him survey my slit.

"You've got a pretty pussy, Natalia. I'll let it rest for a while before I have more of it."

"Yes, sir," I say, then close my eyes, as he carries me to the bed.

CHAPTER EIGHT

HIM & US

*E*dge Beaumont is a man of his word, keeping his promise to defile me and enjoy me as he pleases. He gives me one hour to rest. I lay naked in his arms, until conversation segues into a lip lock of passionate kisses, and a repeat of everything he's done to me—*everything*.

He lies on top of me, kissing me slowly, palming the meat of my breast in a gentle circle.

'Fuck, that feels good.'

I squirm below him, then part my legs so he can rest between them.

Internally I shout, *'Just put it in. Please put it in.'*

I'm wound up like a toy, panting heavily as I refrain from exposing my eagerness, and newfound addiction for him and his cock.

'I'm going to have to detox from this night when it's over.'

My hands have to touch him. They wrap around his shoulders and massage the top of his back. His mouth journeys south to my nipples now raised in his fingertips. He grazes the left one with his teeth, flicking the right one with his finger.

I shiver and sigh. "Ah, my pussy wants you inside."

"Patience, sweet girl. You'll get your wish."

The grazing turns to nibbles and small bites. My pussy vibrates against his hard cock jumping next to my skin.

Edge snickers. "Humph. That pretty pussy can't wait to be beaten."

He lifts up and hovers over me. I could bite him for making me wait two years to enjoy the bond we are creating as I fall prey to his authority. Worshiping his manliness. Yearning his sexual prowess.

He grabs the base of his cock. It putters against my orifice and my hidden lips pulse like a juicer.

Edge pats his shroomhead on my wet folds. "Yes. Aah yes. I could watch you beg for me all day," he whispers at my pussy convulsing with anticipation, tapping my saturated slit like a drum.

The tip rolls around my entrance, teasing me. My hood jumps trying to grab it and lock it inside.

Edge licks his fingers then pats my clit. I wail at the sensation of his head edging in, and the pitter-patter of his flicks beating against me all at once.

His eyes hold mine as he opens my folds with one hand, still tapping my clit with the other.

Pat, pat.

He stops, weakening me with an intense gaze.

I convulse, connecting with him on a deeper level.

Pat, pat.

He stops and my pussy spits cream on the bed.

"Ooooh," he groans and breaks our bonding moment, and slides down for a closeup. "I fucking love that shit." He kisses it like he's sampling icing on a cupcake. "Your pussy just submitted to me. You're mine, sweet girl."

His words, his actions, and his mind games have total control of my psyche. *I am* his. I don't have to verbally say it. My body has exposed my secret, and I can't hide from my truth.

He squeezes my clit with the right precision, lightly licking it with the tip of his tongue.

I scream. "Yes, I am yours!" flying high above the moon in my mind.

The pleasure he awards me is tortuous and stimulating. A finger enters my shuddering hole gently. I'm being squeezed at the clit, licked on the tip, and finger fucked in my slit. My back raises and my ass lifts. Edge slides another finger below my hole and rubs my track as far as his finger will go.

"Don't stop. Please don't stop," I moan.

"Oh, but I must, princess. I still have to fuck those pouring pink walls."

He forges inside, and my walls grip his cock. He breaks free of my hold with a stroke to the end of my tunnel, twisting his head into a corner, beating that spot like a punching bag, grinding into it like he felt at home.

I screech with gratifying agony while looking down at his hips as they swirl around inside my love.

He withdraws, then licks my lips and both nipples. My feet fly above my head, and Edge presses on the back of my thighs. His tongue curves outside of his mouth and pecks inside my pussy, switching to circular licks, clit flicks, then direct pecks in and out of my hole.

Holding me in a buck, he sticks his dick deep inside then pulls it out. My slit stretches open for him and retracts, wanting him to return inside. He obliges, drilling deep to dig for more white gold. He pulls out again and smiles.

"What is it?" I ask, pulling on his thigh.

"It's like watching a flower bloom," he says. "I've swollen your cunt, sweet girl." He kisses my quivering, gaped whole.

I sigh at the softness of his lips. He pulls me upright, holds my chin and kisses me, then shoves his cock in my mouth. I taste myself, and a hint of salt while he fucks my face wild and rough.

Spit gushes from the sides of my mouth as I relax my throat.

"Good girl," he praises me, pulling my hair back to look at my face. He taps his cock on my lips, and they open for him. "One more time, baby. Let me feel the toys in that throat."

I do as he wishes, tearing up at the fucking of my inexperienced oral path. He wipes them, but presses on until I pull away and gasp loudly.

"Tell me your swollen pussy misses me."

I exclaim in a whisper. "My swollen pussy misses you."

"Turn around."

A smack bounces off of my ass then my hair is wrapped around his fist. His cock pommels my swollen hole until it hurts, and squishes come on his cock with each stroke, sputtering in waves while he howls of early morning delight.

He sticks his thumb in my ass. "Keep coming on my dick, Angel."

I murmur, "I can't stop coming. It feels so good it hurts."

"Daddy's got a filthy little angel on his hands." He smacks my ass harder this time before he wiggles his thumb deeper past my entrance.

The lights flicker above us. Power is being restored

in the city as I'm being drained of the little energy I have left. Edge pulls my hair so tight, I feel a crick in my neck while his warm seed shoots from his engorged cock.

The explosion sends chills up my spine. My shoulders cave. The arch in my back locks. He releases me, and we fall side by side on the bed covered in sweat, come, and spit.

Breathless, we listen to each other sigh and grunt. His hand slides down to my slit and holds it with a firm grip until I fall weak and pass out.

I WAKE in the arms of my pussy pulverizer sleeping peacefully halfway under the covers. I leave him to rest while I shower, then return to the room.

My zipper jams. "Dammit," I mumble.

He turns and gets tangled in the sheets. "You weren't going to skip out on me, were you?"

"Of course not."

He pats the bed. "Stay for at least another hour. Or let me take you to breakfast since the city is back online. I know you're hungry because I'm starved."

"I need to find a flight home, so I should get going."

"No need. I gave my travel agent instructions to find us a way to Illinois."

"Us?"

"Yes. Us."

"Edge, we haven't spoken in a year. Were you planning on spending Christmas at my house again this year?"

He nods. "You seem surprised. Your parents didn't

buy that big new house to not show it off for the holidays."

I scoff. "So what do we do now?"

"I would say get in a third round until we get the call. But since you've showered, I'll do the same, and feed your pretty ass. Fingers crossed it gets you refueled for another go."

9

CHAPTER NINE

CHRISTMAS EVE

Our flight lands in the brisk air of Chicago. Edge orders separate cars to deliver us to Aurora, and I arrive at my parent's house hours before him.

Guests enter the new house in droves while I change into my holiday attire. Chatter over the Christmas music playing on the speaker system my father has installed fills the house with an upbeat, happy vibe for the occasion.

I hang back in my room, looking out of the window as the street and yard fill with cars. When Lily pulls up, I ease my way into the crowd downstairs, and greet our old neighbors, my parent's colleagues, and a slew of new faces from the neighborhood.

Lily pulls me into a corner to play catch up with her crazy adventures. As she makes me laugh about her continued college drama into the world of a reverse harem, Edge arrives, and I am dismayed—Calliope is on his arm.

'This motherfucker. He made no mention of her while his cock was shoved down my throat and up my ass.'

Our eyes meet and I cut him with an icy look.

His face turns red with guilt. He looks away from me and blends into the party while I mask my blood boiling with laughs at Lily's bold move to bring her two lovers home for the holidays.

She introduces them to me. "Paul and Sergio, this is my best friend, Nat."

"Can I borrow one for the evening?" I kid.

"They are trained and loyal, honey. Neither of them will step out on our agreement."

The three of them stare at each other.

I lean forward. "I may have to ask you for lessons, Lily. You have two men worshiping you, while I seem to run them off."

"Not for long. I ran into Dante, and he's vowed to win you back."

I huff. "Tell me you're joking."

"I'm not. He's over there winning your mother's approval as we speak."

I look up and see Dante pouring his charm on my mother. "Excuse me."

I snake my way around the party, and hide behind a cluster of my father's partners when the front door opens. Toran enters with presents and the good energy he possesses. I stare at the scruff on his face, admiring how he's changed and grown in our time apart. The facial hair gets a rise out of me, giving him an appeal I find myself swooning over.

I maneuver around the loud talking men and make myself seen. Toran and I smile at each other, and speak without words across the crowded room, then wander into each other's arms.

"I miss you," he says, humming in my ear as he sniffs my neck.

I look over his shoulder at Edge leering at us. "I miss you, too."

Dad pulls him away and introduces him as my boyfriend to his colleagues. I take the time to collect myself, and disappear into my father's study.

As I'm catching my breath, Edge slips in and closes the door behind him.

I smack his face. "You neglected to tell me you're still engaged."

"And you neglected to mention you're still seeing my nephew."

"I'm just as surprised to see him as you are."

Edge grips my face. "Consider Calliope history. I'm breaking it off with her. She's not the woman I want."

"I don't believe you."

"This may sound foolish, but I want to tell Sy about us. You are of age and we wouldn't have to hide."

"He'll kill you and me."

His hands palm my ass. "So, you don't want to keep doing what we did for the past twenty-four hours?"

"I do, I mean I did, until I saw *California* hanging on your arm."

He chuckles. "Calliope is a mild formality. I swear I'm going to take care of it." He kisses my lips, then wipes away my red lipstick. "You are addictive, Ms. Sutton. Stop pretending that bruised pussy doesn't belong to me." He closes his eyes and inhales. "I wish I could feel how swollen it is right now. Pink, pretty, and fat. Is it throbbing for me?"

"Good-bye, Edge." I reveal a sly smile, concealing that I'm yearning for him to defile me once again.

"Want me to call you?"

I nod. "Yes. You knew I wasn't going to say no."

He leaves me in the study as I spiral in my confusion, giving him headway to merge into the party before me.

I find Toran in a deep stare down competition with Dante, and my mother playing referee between the two. Toran latches onto my hand, and clings to me all night. Hours pass with us dancing and mingling until we find a secluded corner to talk.

He's unaware, but I chuckle to myself as sneering eyes judge us from different angles of the room.

He convinces me to give him a second chance with the promise to take it slow, and agrees to my terms to date openly for a while, before becoming exclusive after we graduate.

I'm chuffed that I have bought myself some time to do as I please without the guilt.

"Your uncle is here. Should we go say hello?" I follow his lead over to Edge, smirking on the side of my mouth.

Edge sneers at me while they hug. "It's good to see you two are still going strong."

"Actually, Nat just decided to give me another chance. I promise I won't fuck it up this time."

Edge mutters, glaring at me with poisonous darts. "Oh. It's serious is it?"

Lily joins our circle with her two lovers on each side. "What are you guys talking about?"

Toran looks at Edge. "I was about to ask my uncle how his Christmas has been?"

"So far, incredible." He glances in my direction. "Especially during the blackout. You have no idea how relaxing it was to be in the darkness. There's so much you can get done without the distractions of a phone, or a laptop, or a television." He turns to Toran and asks, "What do you want Saint Nick to bring you, nephew?"

Toran looks at me. "I already have it."

"And you?" Edge asks me.

"I didn't ask for anything in particular this year. Whatever I get will be a complete surprise."

"A woman like that is a keeper, nephew. I would know."

I choke on his audacity. "Where is *Canopy?*"

Edge scoffs. "Calliope is somewhere around here."

I giggle to myself and look around the room at the drunk faces, blitzed enjoying the holiday. Surrounded by two amazing men, I realize Lily may need to advise me sooner than later.

I think to myself, *'What should I call Edge and Toran? Lovers, fuck buddies, friends with benefits. Pound pals perhaps.'* I smile when *The NET,* flashes in my head. "Natalia, Edge, & Toran."

Lily whispers in my ear. "I didn't know you were back with the horn blower. Somebody is keeping secrets."

"I have so much to tell you," I giggle. "And trust me when I say, no one would understand more than you."

She glances at Toran. "Does that mean you got what you wanted for Christmas?"

"I got what I wanted and more," I answer her, when the thought crosses my mind, *'And I plan on keeping them both. At least for a little while.'*

A
VERY
MERRY
Xmess
DIANNE JUNE

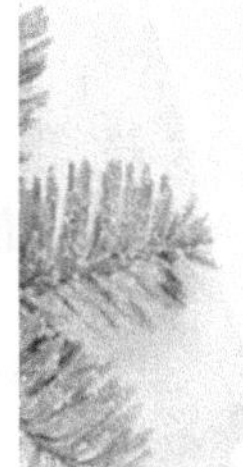

PLEASE LEAVE A REVIEW
AND
CHECK OUT MY OTHER
QUICK READS

I WOULD GREATLY
APPRECIATE IT

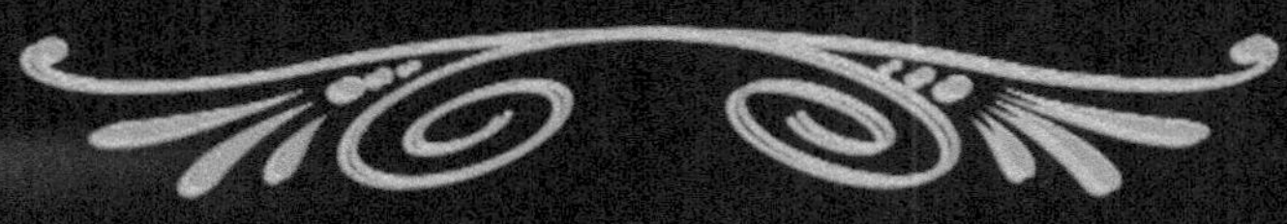

DJ

QUICK LINKS

Sign up for my newsletter for more content, contests & giveaways here: https://diannejune.ck.page & stay up to date with group chats and news inside my reader group here:

www.facebook.com/groups/diannesdiehards

Follow me on social for visual content and to stay in touch on the following sites:

https://www.tiktok.com/@authordiannejune
https://www.instagram.com/authordiannejune/

STEAMY READS
BY
DIANNE JUNE

AVAILABLE
ON KU

CURRENTLY
ON
KINDLE
VELLA

STEAMY
XMAS

AVAILABLE
EVERYWHERE &
IN PRINT

www.ingramcontent.com/pod-product-compliance
Lightning Source LLC
Chambersburg PA
CBHW071433300726
48976CB00004B/1319